Three Rivers Rising

Jame Richards

Three Rivers Rising

A Novel of the Johnstown Flood

Alfred A. Knopf ✦ New York

THIS IS A BORZOI BOOK PUBLISHED BY ALFRED A. KNOPF

Visit us on the Web! www.randomhouse.com/teens

Educators and librarians, for a variety of teaching tools, visit us at www.randomhouse.com/teachers

Library of Congress Cataloging-in-Publication Data
Richards, Jame.
Three rivers rising : a novel of the Johnstown flood / Jame Richards. — 1st ed.
      p. cm.
Summary: Sixteen-year-old Celestia is a wealthy member of the South Fork Fishing and Hunting Club, where she meets and falls in love with Peter, a hired hand who lives in the valley below, and by the time of the torrential rains that lead to the disastrous Johnstown flood, she has been disowned by her family and is staying with him in Johnstown. Includes an author's note and historical timeline.
Includes bibliographical references.

ISBN 978-0-375-85885-7 (trade) — ISBN 978-0-375-95885-4 (lib. bdg.) —
ISBN 978-0-375-89553-1 (e-book)
1. Floods—Pennsylvania—Johnstown (Cambria County)—Juvenile fiction. [1. Floods—Pennsylvania—Johnstown (Cambria County)—Fiction. 2. Social classes—Fiction.] I. Title.
PZ7.R3846Th 2010
[Fic]—dc22
2009004251

The text of this book is set in 11-point Goudy.

Printed in the United States of America
April 2010
10 9 8 7 6 5 4 3 2 1
First Edition

Random House Children's Books supports the First Amendment and celebrates the right to read.

to Mom and Dad,
to Grace and Frances Mae,
and to Franny

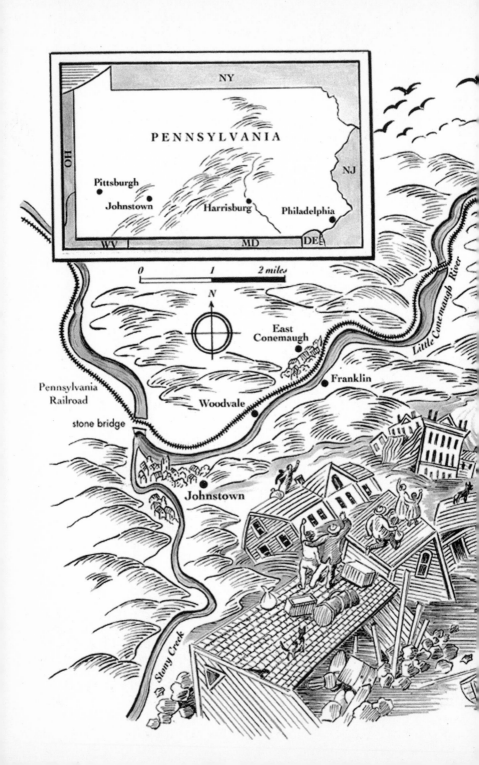

THE PATH OF THE JOHNSTOWN FLOOD
1889

Mineral Point

Little Conemaugh River

• South Fork

South Fork Creek

South Fork Dam

clubhouse

Lake
Conemaugh

SUMMER SEASON

1888

South Fork Fishing and Hunting Club
Lake Conemaugh

Celestia

Father says he comes for the fishing,
but in truth he comes to keep an eye
on other businessmen.
I have never seen him hook
a worm or tie a fly.
I cannot imagine him gutting a fish
or scraping scales.
The only scales he knows
are for banking and shipping.
But his partners and rivals decided
it was time for fresh air,

exercise,
peace and quiet,
away from the filth and crowds of the city.
So, even at this pastoral lakeside resort,
my father will not miss
the glimmer of a business deal
spoken over rifles or fishing reels.

Mother likes the sociability of the other ladies
though they cut her with their tongues.
She does not always follow their jokes
but laughs along.
The gentlemen come to hunt animals;
the ladies come to hunt other ladies
of a weaker sort.

Estrella shines—
glossy dark eyelashes
and smooth pink cheeks.
My parents' favorite,
and, at nineteen, my senior by three years.
She starts each day in a steamer chair
with plaid blankets and a book.
She plays the part of the lovesick sweetheart—
her beau, Charles, learns the family business
back home in Pittsburgh—
but her natural buoyancy is not long repressed.
Fun always knows where to find her.

Just now, an errant croquet ball rolls under her chair.
She laughs and runs to the game,
the dappled sunlight,
and the jovial golden boys.
Handsome Frederick
meets her halfway,
extending his arm.
Frederick with his shock of blond hair,
broad shoulders,
and skin glowing with health . . .
Poor old Charles
with his consumptive cough
better arrive soon
if he wants to find his intended still betrothed.
He cannot compete with the gaiety
and romance of our sparkling little lake in the mountains.

Now about me—
if I am not the fun-loving beauty,
then I must be the serious one,
the one who would toss the croquet ball back,
wave and sigh,
but be infinitely more fascinated
with my book
than with the superficial cheer
of the society crowd.
The one who gets the joke
but does not tolerate it.

The one who baits the hook
and guts the fish
with Peter,
the hired boy.

Peter

Papa says, "It's unnatural—
lakes weren't meant to be
so high in the mountains,
up over all our heads.
Rich folks think
they know better than God
where a lake oughta be."

He's talking about South Fork Reservoir,
miles of icy creek water
held in place above our valley
by a seventy-foot earthen dam.

The owners call it Lake Conemaugh.
They raised it up from a puddle,
built fancy-trim houses all in a row
and a big clubhouse on the shore,
stocked it with fish,
and now they bring their families in from Pittsburgh
every summer season.

Most of them stay in the clubhouse,
like an oversized hotel
with wide hallways,
a huge dining room,
and a long front porch
across the whole thing.
Dozens of windows, too,
so every room has a view
of the reservoir—
I mean, the lake.

Papa says, "They can't stack up enough money
against all that water."

"Oh, Papa." I wave off the idea.
Everybody in Johnstown
kids each other about the dam breaking.
We laugh because it always holds.
Papa says we're laughing off our fear.
Folks think he's something of a crank
for always bringing it up.

I don't say anything more—
at least until I can think how to tell him
the sportsmen's club
up at the reservoir
is my new boss.

Papa says, "Don't go up there.
Being around all those rich folks'll only give you ideas
of things you can't have."

He looks at Mama's picture.
I know he's thinking of ideas she had
for things he couldn't give her.
That was before she went to rest underground
in the cemetery on the hill.

Papa works underground
in a different hill,
digging coal for the Cambria Iron Works.
Papa says the mines are graveyards, too,
only without the resting and the peace.
His tears are black
and his cough is black.

I try not to smile. "I bet I won't hardly see
any rich folks,
they'll have me working so hard,
planting
and pruning
and lugging stuff around."
I see him considering but
I pretend to give in.
"Oh, okay, Papa, I'll just come to work with you, then.
Ask the foreman to find me a spot on the line."

He shakes his head,
coughing over his grumbling.
"No, you go up where the air is clean."
We both know,
now that I've turned sixteen,
I'll be in the mills soon enough,
putting in ten-hour days or more
on the Iron Works payroll.
Why not have one last summer of sun and fish?

He packs me a lunch bucket
with enough for several meals
and hands me his good wax coat.

Papa walks me to the edge of town,
our boots nearly left behind with each step
on this slop of a road.
Mud is just
part of life
in the valley.
Johnstown sits at the junction
of the Stony Creek
and the Little Conemaugh River,
which is joined—
above us, to the east—
by the South Fork Creek
after it fills the reservoir.
Due to the sometimes quicksilver activity

of these three rivers
after heavy rainfall,
Johnstown is no stranger to spring floods.

Papa claps his arm
on my shoulder
in place of goodbyes.
He looks like he wants to say something,
to say a lot of things,
if he could,
but we just look up the mountain pass together.

Right here where we're standing
a long-ago river flowed,
carving a deep channel
through the rocks and mountains,
paying no mind
to the wildflowers that'd grow
someday,
or the little wooden towns
that'd spring up in the valley,
or the miner and his son
and the words they can and can't say.

The shadow of that old-time river
ripples over us,
and I leave Papa behind
on the road.

Celestia

How might a girl like me,
who loves only books,
find herself wrist-deep in fish entrails?
With a boy
not of her rank?

It all began with the need for quiet,
a place to read
without the insufferable incessant prattling
of Mrs. Godwin
and that vicious little wig with teeth
she calls a dog.

I scouted a mossy glade
near one of the feeder streams,
relishing the exercise
but, even more, enjoying the solitude.

A rule must have been declared
at Lake Conemaugh
that no one leaves you alone for long
when you are enjoying yourself.
So about the third time the hired boy, Peter,
walked by with his fishing pole,
I spoke up: "The fish not biting today?"
"Well"— he looked at his shoes—
"this used to be my favorite spot."

I thought it was only fair
to invite him to set up here,
though Mother would have fits
if she knew I was ten feet away
from a strange boy
without a chaperone in sight.
And without a parasol—
she begs me not to freckle.

Unlikely that anyone would happen by
and report my transgressions to her,
so I took a chance.

Peter

I told myself it was the sun
playing tricks on my eyes,
that fancy rich girls all in white
don't sit around between tree roots
on the muddy banks of a creek.

So I went back
to look again.

And there she was.
Like she belonged there.
Gave me that feeling

like when you see
the first snowflake of winter:
You knew it'd come eventually,
but you're still taken by surprise.
And you look at it,
hard as you can,
for that second
before it melts,
because you never want to forget it.
It's one of a kind.
And it reminds you how every leaf,
every tree,
every everything
is one of a kind.
And you always knew it,
only maybe you stopped noticing it
so much.

I just looked
hard as I could
at this one-of-a-kind girl
like she was gonna melt
and I didn't want to forget her.

My mouth went dry
and I think I dropped my fishing pole.

She spotted me
and smiled.

Celestia

Curiosity led me back
the next day.
And the next.
Each day he ambled by
and acted surprised to see me.
Each day I smiled into my book
and sneaked looks over the page tops.

"Would you mind very much, Miss,
if I turned up my sleeves?" Peter puts down his bucket and pole.
"Not at all. The sun is quite warm today." I look away discreetly,
but I see without quite looking
as he unfastens one cuff
and rolls the fabric up to the elbow.
Then the other.
When he takes up the rod again
I finally glance:
forearms
sun brown
like bread baking
in a hot oven.

The sun has heated me through.
My eyelids feel heavy
and I am dreaming of a warm golden hand
tracing the curve of my face.
A sigh escapes me.

"That must be some book!" Peter's voice jostles me awake.
"Oh . . . yes." My cheeks turn to flames.
"The sun might be too much for you today, Miss.
I can see from here you're red."
"You are right. I should go." I start for the trees,
stopping to steal one more glance
to hold me over until next time. . . .
Will there be a next time?

He stands with one foot on a rock,
leaning on his bended knee,
watching me.
When I turn, he laughs.

"Tomorrow?" He straightens.
I feel utterly exposed.
Looking straight on
at a boy,
and him at me.
Alone.
I nod.
"Tomorrow."

Peter fishes,
I read,
mostly in silence.

Soon I read a few pages aloud,
reclining on a rock,
one hand trailing in the cool water.
When I look up from my book,
he is staring right into my eyes,
apparently unaware of the fish tugging at his line.

I cannot look away either,
but I suppress a smile.
"It appears you need some help."
I stand and reach
for the line,
revealing a
wriggling fish
glinting in the sun.
I look up at him. "What now?"
His face is close.
"I'll show you."

After the fishing lesson,
I hand Peter my book in trade.
He must perceive some hesitation.
"I *can* read." He pulls the book toward him.
"I . . . I never said . . . "
"I went to school."
"Of course."
"My mother was a schoolteacher," he says,
"before she married."

"A teacher—what could be more wonderful?"
"She was sad to leave it, so I became her pupil.
She'd traveled, brought back dozens of books.
She started to teach me Latin, but . . .
well, she's been gone a long time now."
Peter looks away.
"I am so sorry. What was her name?"
"Anna."
"Were you very young?"
Peter nods. "Any age would've been too young."

As the summer sun intensifies,
our conversations follow suit,
many of them conducted
while treading water
in the furthest recesses of the reservoir.

No artifice,
no pretending to faint
or slipping so he could catch me.
Just our locked gaze
tightening the space between us
until our voices
need only whisper,
lips to ear,
then lips upon lips.

⸙

We instinctively know to hide our meetings,
to never speak of them to others.

When we cross paths—
me strolling the boardwalks with my mother,
him weeding a border—
we do not exchange longing glances.
The risk would be too great.

The eyes of every busybody
in the club
are on me.
And Peter's hawk-eyed supervisor
wrings him out
for every drop of work.
Even the suspicion of fraternizing
with a guest
would be grounds for dismissal.

There will be no romantic picnic outings
to the waterfall for us.
Only brief afternoon swims
and furtive moments in the dark woods.

"Was anyone watching you leave?"
Peter steers me into a hollow
between the trees.
I look over my shoulder,
scan the horizon. "No, I was careful.

My parents . . .
you know they would not approve?"
"My pop, too, said don't come up here."
Peter looks down at me
and laces his fingers
in my hair. "He didn't want me
to develop a taste for things I can't have."
I hold his wrists. "But you do have me, Peter."
"For now." He grins.
"For always . . . if you want me."

"We both know that could never be, Celestia.
Forsake your family?
You love them."
"I do love them,
and I do not relish the thought
of defying them,
but we can find a way
someday.
We must try."

"I couldn't ask you to give up this kind of life. . . ."
Peter shrugs toward the clubhouse.
"I want you to ask me."—I grab his shoulders—
"Say it.
Say you want me for always
and I will weather the storm,
whatever comes."
I have pulled him slightly closer,

19

causing his hands
to release my combs.
A spark travels up my spine
and I watch his face
as he lets his fingers fall with my hair.
He uncoils it to the end,
all the way down my back,
until, his face on my neck,
his breath in my ear: "Celestia"—
his arms tighten around me—
"for always, of course."

No one can know.
Yet
the color in my cheeks
and the bubbling in my speech
are not lost on Estrella,
serene at her stitching
but glancing from under those long lashes,
again and again,
biting her lips
to hide a smile.
Finally I become flustered
and throw my mess
of tangled thread aside. "Oh, for heaven's sake!"
She bursts out laughing
and I cannot help but laugh, too.

She sees through me
and I am glad.
"Let us talk
after everyone has gone to bed," she whispers,
eyeing the doorway
through which Mother and the maid can be heard.
"Come to my room, then," I say,
handing her my needle and frame.
"Just like old times." Estrella hums
and picks at my mangled stitches.

Not so long ago,
we shared a room at home.
When I was small and afraid of the dark,
she wrapped her arms around me, saying,
"You do not have to be brave.
I will be brave for both of us."
When I was older and reading half the night,
she just pulled the blankets over her head,
saying, "Tell me the story in the morning."
I found I enjoyed telling the stories
almost as much as reading them.
Estrella laughed in all the right places
and sighed at the end,
"I cannot wait to hear what follows.
How will I ever survive until tomorrow?"

"You can guess I have a story for you."
I unravel a knot of floss

to keep from giggling.
Estrella blushes.
"And I might just have a story *for you* as well."

We compose ourselves
as Mother returns.

⚬～✹～⚬

Cozy in my featherbed—
the softest knock can only be
Estrella
in her nightdress,
a long braid
and bare feet.
She skips like a stone
scarcely touching the floor
before leaping onto my bed.
I catch her in my quilt
and we snuggle under.

"I know there's something going on.
Don't try to deny it." Estrella pokes me in the ribs.
"Are you a gossip now?" I give her the tiniest pinch,
sharper that way. "Are you minion to Mrs. Godwin?"
"Ow!" She swats my hand away. "Just tell me. Is it a boy?"
"Maybe."
"Which one. I can find out. You may as well tell me."
"He is not who you might expect."

"Hmm. Is he older? Younger? Ugly?" She tugs my hair.
"Sit up. You cannot sleep with your hair in disarray."
Estrella sets to sectioning my hair for a braid like hers.
I had left it loose,
savoring the sensation of Peter's hands in it.
"He works here." My hair goes slack.
I turn to face my sister.
She does not blink.
Her cheeks have gone white.
"Do not judge me, Estrella."
"I do not." She looks away. "You know the risks
as well as I do.
A terribly high price is to be paid
when a young lady of society
falls in love
with the wrong man."
"That is why it must remain a secret."
"Of course." She turns me around by my shoulders
and returns to braiding my hair.

Tap.
Estrella and I look around.
Tap.
It comes from the window.
Tap.
A pebble strikes the glass.

I go to the window.
Moonlight casts a shadow
of every leaf
dancing in the breeze,
and the figure beneath the tree
can only be
Peter.
I wave.

"The window in the sitting room
opens onto the porch roof"—Estrella has gathered
the quilt around herself
and picked up my book,
as if our conversation were officially ended—
"just an arm's length from the tree
that grows alongside."
"Oh?"
She casually turns a page.
I reach for a wrap
and I suddenly think,
How does she know so much about sneaking out?
She looks so engrossed in that book.

As I throw one leg over the sill
I remember she said she had a story to tell *me*. . . .
Oh well—it can wait until breakfast.

Peter

I admit I'm disappointed
when Celestia turns
from the window so quickly.
But I keep looking up anyway,
making do with the space
she used to fill.

The leaves rustle—
almost feels like she's near—
maybe it's just the breeze.
But no,
she's touching my sleeve.
How did she get here?
Can't help myself—I pull her close
and she covers her mouth
to hold in her laugh.
I move her hand away
but I don't kiss her.
Not yet.

⟨✿⟩

I grab Celestia's hand
and we run for the dam,
waiting to let loose
our laughter
until we're out of earshot of the clubhouse.

We stop on the crest,
wobbly legged
and out of breath.

"I wonder if it's bad luck
to stand on the dam." I sidearm a flat stone,
three hops across the lake surface.
"Why? Are you scared?"
Celestia makes her eyes go wide,
and nudges me with her shoulder.

"Nah. Just wonder if it's tempting fate."
"Maybe we should stop talking—
landslides you know," Celestia whispers
with a wink. She glances downhill
and moves closer to me.
My arms are around her in a second.

With Lake Conemaugh on one side
and the valley of my home on the other,
we stand on the border,
locked in a kiss
that makes sense of it all.

To my mind,
a clear night sky
with a sugaring of stars,

enormous and
silent as a snowfall,
that's the only church we need.

I used to think
I could see straight up to heaven
if I looked hard enough.
Mama'd be holding out her arms,
smelling like sunshine
and honey.
And me, so small
and alone in the dark . . .
But she could find me,
love like a thread between us.

That's how it is
to be with Celestia—
standing in a church of stars,
feeling so small,
and letting love
find me anyway.

Celestia

He says I remind him of maps of constellations
on a sapphire background.
No one ever thought of me as magic before,

as sacred.
"My name is giving you ideas"—I laugh and splash,
gathering my shift around my legs
to wade into one of the feeder creeks above the lake—
"and this is you, then."
I balance a striped river rock on my palm.
He looks down at mud and dirt,
frowning.
"And this"—I hand him a smooth marled stone—
"and this," an oxblood red.

"Your name means rock," I say.
Peter studies each one
and smiles. "I never thought of that
as a good thing,
but these are great.
Why didn't I ever notice before?
Hey, this one's nearly green."
We dive for rocks,
collecting them in the hem of my skirts
draped over a low branch.

Later, when I arrive for dinner
still damp,
everyone turns
toward the sound,
a young girl
clattering like river rocks.

I suppose I have always had that effect,
the fur of the cat rubbed wrong.
Mrs. Godwin wiggles her ear
by its diamond festoon
and returns to *tink-tink-tinking* her orange pekoe.
Only the surly little dog
seems to understand
that my music is not his imagination.
He licks my silty ankles
and nips my dripping petticoats,
snarling,
tugging,
smelling frogs, perhaps,
until his mistress scolds him back to her lap.

Mother pales
and whispers through a strained smile,
"I do not know how to make clear to you children
the necessity of proper decorum . . .
oh, I'm fairly swooning in this heat.
When will your father ever arrive from Pittsburgh?"
Estrella hands over her fan,
which distracts Mother from her chatter—
she fans herself
and watches the other diners.

Estrella turns to me
and smiles warmly,
truly looks at me.

She winks
and pours steaming tea
in my cup,
ceremoniously,
as if I were a queen.

Sundown.
A breeze off the lake
finds its way to me
through the open windows
of the dining room.
Hot tea notwithstanding,
I am covered in gooseflesh.
Mother stutters in protest
as I excuse myself,
no more than two bites
into the main course.

Turning the corner
onto the landing,
I plow into a dark coat and starched collar,
knocking the hat off a gentleman's head.
He grabs my arm as I stumble back down a stair,
safe,
but his black bowler
bumps down

step
after
step.

I recognize Father's colleague, Mr. Grayson—
younger,
richer,
the word "tycoon"
always following his name in the papers.
I stammer an apology.
"Miss Celestia?" Grayson appraises
my dampened state
head to toe
for far too long. "A bit late in the day
for swimming,
wouldn't you say?"

Aunt Mimsy, Mother's sharp-witted sister,
says he has ruined girls
in New York and Milan.
She calls him "silver-tongued
and handsome as the devil."
She says he stinks of new money.
This always makes me wonder
how much newer
his could be
than ours.

I move out of his grasp
and his gaze
to hurry down the hall.
Is it laughter I hear
before he whistles his way down the stairs
twirling that silly walking stick?

East Conemaugh

Maura

He's a good man, Joseph.
I watch him while he snores,
with his thatch of copper-red hair
and thick freckled arms.
He's given me three babies now
and me not through my seventeenth year.
I keep them quiet with rag toys
when he's asleep,
though he's good-natured enough
with their mischief,
hoisting them on his shoulders and jigging.

He rises and drinks his coffee scalding like lead,
like the hot metal they use to make the rails he rides.

It must be in his veins,
coursing through
the way
he brings the big engine down
the Conemaugh line.

His embrace lifts my feet off the ground.
He chucks my chin like the children's
but his kiss is only for a wife.

He turns and waves.
I lean into the door frame.

How can a house full of babies feel empty?
My heart keeps time
with the mantel clock
until I hear that train whistle again.
He pulls an extra blast as they near the station
and I know it is just for me,
to tell all the world he loves me,
to tell me he can't wait to come home.

Pennsylvania Railroad

Kate

Years back they called me Kitty.
Vain as any.
Spent hours plaiting my hair.
Spent pennies on ribbons.
Foolishness.

I had certain talents, though:
fixing up Mum's pantry,
everything labeled and in reach;
scheduling the family chores
so we didn't trip each other coming and going.
And the pies!
Those berry pies won Best in Fair since I was big enough

to put my back into the rolling pin.
But that's all pride,   .
gone long ago.

Pride of the county,
everyone said,
Kitty will make one heck of a wife someday.
Of all the farm girls, none can beat her.
And Early Becker was one for thinking ahead.

We made plans,
Early and me,
right there
in the schoolyard.
"A girl who can see the natural order of things
is the perfect bride for me."
Spoken for
and not even in long skirts yet.

He'd thought it all out,
explained
what I was agreeing to:
the crops,
the animals,
changes over how his daddy did things.
He promised he'd never tire of me—
hair and freckles the color of milky tea.
Together, there wasn't anything could beat us.
And I agreed.

Years later,
a picnic
by the stream.
Doubled back to the springhouse
for cream for the pie.
While I was gone,
must be Early slipped,
the kind of thing we would have laughed about later,
only he hit his head on a rock
and went out cold in the water.
When I got back,
pulled him up on the bank,
didn't know how to make him breathe,
mostly just screamed.

Wish that day
could be undone.
Lost Early.
Lost Kitty—
replaced her with Kate,
just plain Kate.

After Early's passing,
the Kate in me took over.
Could not stop myself—
swept and washed and polished
around the farm

until Mum and Daddy could stand it no more.
Could not rest,
and the family clothes could not endure
even one more vigorous scrubbing.

A few necessities packed—
nothing can give a body comfort
when your own life is what torments you—
and now Daddy hitches the team
and drives us to the train.

This need for cleaning and counting and organizing
will better serve me as a nurse in training.

"Don't wait." I stare straight ahead at the tracks.
Daddy nods and peers toward the treetops.
"Looks like rain,"
his way of saying
all that a man can't say,
squinting so his eyes don't shine.
I gather my things and jump down quickly
so he can go.
He shouldn't see his only daughter take this step
into an unwelcome destiny,
something to pass the time until death,
until she joins Early.

South Fork Fishing and Hunting Club
Lake Conemaugh

Peter

"There ain't no future in it," Papa had said
between coughs
when I brought him a basket of fish
one Sunday. "This girl's sired
and milk-fed
for the one purpose
of getting herself a rich husband—
like all them society girls.
You mess with that,
her daddy'll make quick work of you."

I pretended to square off and throw a few punches.
"Maybe I'll be found
at the bottom of the lake one day
if they ever drain it."
Papa didn't laugh.

He looked at me straight,
his eyes tired. "She pretty?"
"And more," I said.
"Like your mother, I bet.
The first crocus always found her.
And she could recite whole poems.
Do you remember?"
I said, "Yes,
a little."
But what I didn't say
is that I mostly remember
her gentle voice
singing to me
in the darkness.
Not her face,
but the smooth of her hands.

Celestia and I wander too far
looking for arrowheads
and those little white flowers

she weaves into a halo.
We hear the *crack crack*.
I drop to the forest floor,
remembering Papa's words
about a rich man holding my life cheap
compared to his daughter's good name.

When I can swallow a breath again: "Hunters."
Celestia hides, too.
The pine needles are warm.
We hear boots shushing through dried leaves.
Voices become clear.

The first voice: "It has rained
every spring
since time began."

The second voice: "The caretaker says
the dam was reinforced years ago."

The third voice: "All I'm saying is,
there are an awful lot of people in that valley."

"You think too much, Stan.
Why don't you just relax?
Think about pheasants."

"Yeah, pheasants, not peasants."

The one they call Stan is quiet.

Then they are gone and the forest is quiet.

Back in Johnstown
we're always joking
about the dam breaking
because it never does.
"Do you think he's right to worry?"

Celestia smoothes my forehead.
"If the dam needed fixing,
they would fix it.
Common sense."

East Conemaugh

Maura

A quick one-two blast
of Joseph's whistle
tells me his engine is pulling into the train yard
and he is eager for his dinner.
I stir the big pot of potatoes
and wish for some variety.

The eldest on my hip,
I put the kettle on for tea.
Joseph's womenfolk can read the leaves in a teacup
the way farmers can read the skies.
I wish they would come
and read a nice bit of mutton in my future,
but, sure enough, they'll read another baby.
My body always runs on schedule
just like the trains.

South Fork Fishing and Hunting Club
Lake Conemaugh

Celestia

Setting out on the trail
one afternoon,
who should I pass coming the other way
but my own dear Estrella.
Her step quick,
her eyes bright,
she looks startled to see me. "Celestia, darling . . ."
I cannot conceal my surprise
at seeing her out walking: "What are you doing
out here all alone?"
She beams and hugs herself. "I thought to take a little turn

about the park since it is such a lovely day,
maybe see the waterfall.
It *is* a splendid day, is it not?"
"The waterfall is the other way." I point toward the dam
where the spillway creates a picturesque picnic spot.
"No mystery, then, why I did not see it.
Enjoy your swim." Estrella winks
and moves past me. "See you at dinner."

I turn to watch her slender frame
traverse the rocks and tree roots
with the same easy grace
as if she were dancing in a candlelit ballroom.
Everything comes so easily to Estrella, I think,
as I have a million times before.
But the quality I admire most
is her lightness of heart.

"It *is* a splendid day," I say to the trees,
trying on Estrella's cheerful tone
as I make my way to Peter.

Well before my intended destination,
I notice a shape moving in the shadows,
one that could only be a man.
Perhaps Peter has changed plans
and come to meet me here.

I am nearly an arm's reach from the figure
before he makes himself fully visible.
"Splendid day, is it not, Miss Celestia."
Grayson!
The young tycoon.

I draw back
and feel my stomach clutch.
Did he say *splendid*?

"What are you doing here?" I ask.
"Hunting. Of course."
"I suppose it would be rude to inquire
as to the whereabouts of your gun."
"Ah, yes, my gun. Where did I leave it?" He smirks
and pats his pockets.

"Where are you off to?" Grayson extends his arm. "Who knows,
perhaps we shall discover my rifle."
"It is my intention to swim.
As a gentleman,
you will understand
my insistence on privacy," I say,
though I know
he is *not* a gentleman.
He reaches for my hand and bows. "As you wish."
He knows he is not a gentleman.

I snatch my hand away and hasten toward Peter.
I refuse to look back
but I hold my breath until I hear
Grayson's irritating trilling tuneless whistle
descend in the distance.

How ever did Estrella get past this man
and still remain in good humor?

Pennsylvania Railroad

Kate

Destination, nursing school.
Standing on the platform at the station.
My mind reviews its list
again
and again:
    arrangements in place,
    the tiny sum of unused wedding money
    wired to the head nurse,
    thick coat,
    warm hat,
    gloves with no holes,
    which should get any girl through a year of study,

though they barely reach the wristbones,
and, of course, a complete meal and two snacks:
    hard-boiled eggs, a hunk of cheese, two heels of bread,
    a bit of ham, and a jar of milk.
    Someone snuck in a wedge of last night's pie.
    Leave it on the bench.
    Pie is not what makes the body go.

No time for mooning and sulking
over what happened to Early
and what's become of me since,
how stiff and aged.
Prepare for the work
and the cold
and the homesickness, should it come—
pride and frailty,
nonsense.

Bring the return ticket
Daddy bought
to the caged window
for a refund.
The cashier pushes the fare
through the glass
without a word.
Home?
Loved it once
but won't be coming back.

South Fork Fishing and Hunting Club
Lake Conemaugh

Celestia

Mother wrings her hands,
paces the drawing room.
"You have always been such a good girl—
perhaps too much at your books,
but still, sensible. . . ."
"What is it, Mother?" I take a step toward her.

"We've provided every opportunity
for you as a young woman,
your schooling, your social activities,
your coming-out cotillion next year,
the right kind of people. . . ."

50

I sigh.

"What is this about, Mother?"

I perch on the arm of a chair,

prepared to wait out the lecture.

"Louise Godwin saw you . . ."

"That old busybody."

". . . with him." Mother pulls her mouth tight

and looks down at me.

I straighten up. "Where?"

"In the lake."

"Oh"—I wave a hand, making light—"swimming.

Am I not permitted to swim?"

"Alone?

With some boy?

You know better!"

"He is not 'some boy.'

He has a name."

"He is not like us, Celestia darling."

"Correct. He earns his keep." I speak through clenched teeth.

Mother arranges her face into a stern look.

"Your father works very hard."

"We all agree that Father works hard.

When *is* he due back from Pittsburgh?"

"About eight, unless he gets a late start—

do not change the subject!

Your father will take this up with you when he returns."

"Father? But how would *he* know?"
"Circumstances forced me to tell him."
"What circumstances?" I search my mother's face,
but it is twisting up with emotion.

Mother drops to her knees,
grabs my shoulders. "*Listen* to him, Celestia.
I beg you.
You have not yet seen the world
the way we have.
Your actions could not only tear us
from our place in society
but rip this family apart,
person from person." Mother throws herself across me
as if I were leaving. "Do not take yourself from me, Celestia,
my precious baby."

I circle my arms round her narrow shoulders,
now heaving as she sobs.
As always, with Mother, I am torn
between protectiveness and impatience.
Her love is a certainty
but her perspective is skewed.
Times have changed since she was a girl.

I enter the front room
where my father attends to business

when he's here.
Darkness.
My eyes adjust.
In the low lamplight,
Father looks tired from his journey.

Before I sit, I hear laughter out on the lake.
A ladylike laugh.
I'm drawn to the window
to peer into the dark.
A couple drifts in a rowboat
strung with glowing lanterns.
Time has stopped for them.
A little island
beyond scrutiny.
The graceful stretch of her arm,
the low timbre of voice . . .
could it be Estrella floating outside of time
with an admirer?

Estrella singing.
To . . . whom?
To handsome Frederick,
with his mop of golden hair
and his affable smile?
Cannot make him out.
Cannot quite catch the tune.

Father rubs his face
and combs the strands of hair over his forehead

with his fingers.
I feel pity for him in the brief moment
before he runs me like his business.

"This nonsense must stop."
Father stares out the window,
hands behind his back.
"You are from a decent family. . . ."
I glance from him to the rowboat.
Is he addressing me or Estrella?

He rocks on his heels. "People have begun to talk."
I settle on the arm of a chair
and pick a briar from my sleeve. "Gossips and windbags."
"These are people whose good opinion we hold in esteem.
Polite society.
Business contacts." Father taps the mahogany desk for emphasis.
I recoil. "I assure you I have done nothing
to besmirch the good name of our family."

Father stops and glares.
His eyes are burning ingots.
"I want you to stay away from the hired boy."
"Why?" My back straightens and I raise my chin.
"I am your father.
I don't have to explain." Father tucks papers into a ledger,
signaling the end of discussion. "It has been arranged for you
to accompany your aunt Mimsy abroad.

You will be her traveling companion
until you begin finishing school in Switzerland."
Indignation rushes heat
through my entire body.
"I will not go!" I am on my feet.
"And I will not stop being friends with Peter."

Father slaps the ledger on the desk.

"I have not worked myself blind all these years
so you can shame me
and live in a dirt-floor shack
in the valley!" Father leans across the desk,
red-faced,
cords standing out on his neck.
"Do you even know what one looks like?
I do. I came from one.
And I turned a pile of nothing into a fortune.
How easy for you to take it for granted!
I suggest you go with your aunt and grow up."

"You cannot fire me like one of your employees!" My voice is
shrill.

His face says otherwise. "If you choose the boy,
then you are no longer my daughter."

The clock strikes many times throughout my packing.
Each item my hands light upon
gives me pause:
Would I take this to Europe with Aunt Mimsy?
Would it comfort me
through the empty affectations of school abroad?
Each book a lifeline,
a certainty that my own blood courses through me
and me alone . . .
Or:
Would I take this to the valley
to live with Peter and his father
and leave behind the only life I know?
Perhaps the brush and mirror with inlaid mother-of-pearl
would not serve me there,
though I know it to be a proper wooden house,
not the dirt-floor shack Father suggests.
I could leave behind the trinkets with ease—
but to leave behind my gentle guileless mother?
My hardworking earnest father?
And, most of all, Estrella
with her tinkling bracelets,
her warm voice,
the way she holds my face in her hands
and looks into my eyes—
she is the only one who ever tried to know me,
the dearest friend of my life
before Peter.

Mimsy arrives just after dinner.
She is resplendent in her picture hat and furs.
Little dogs patter on either side
and an entourage of people and luggage and commotion
follows in her wake,
though she is serene as the lake without wind.

Mimsy bats her eyes at me and demands a kiss.
I smile—it is impossible not to smile in her presence—
and rush into her arms.
Her embrace is long and sweet.
She smells of lemongrass.

I can feel my forgiveness.
No, Mimsy is not to blame.
She is merely the vehicle
through which my parents have planned my removal.
She is a delightful consolation. If only
I did not have to remind myself
that I am not choosing Peter.

Peter

Her aunt's coming for her.
Nothing to be done.
The summer days that stretched out before us
snapped back
and slapped our wrists.
Nothing to be done.

She gives me little things to keep,
to remember her by—
glass,
porcelain—
"breakables," she calls them.
"What do people do with them?"
"Nothing, just show how fancy they are
that they can keep them from breaking, I guess."
I'll put one in each pocket,
so they don't smash each other.
Fancy.

I give her my favorite river rocks,
the ones she found for me:
striped,
green,
oxblood,
speckled.

We hold them up next to each other—
the breakables and the rocks.

"The finest faceted crystal comes from sand," she says.
I don't know why we're talking about this
in our last moments,
we just can't make ourselves say goodbye.
"The sheerest porcelain
you can see light through
comes from clay," she says,
"and the purest diamond comes from coal."
I pull her closer. "Everything comes from something."
"Exactly"—she touches my cheek—
"the distance between them . . .
is time."
"Or alchemy." I tear my eyes away from her face
to look off down the valley.

The sunset competes with the red glow over Johnstown.
And I know,
at any given moment,
metal is liquid fire
lighting the night sky,
becoming steel
that will build tracks
to anywhere she might be.
It will build bridges between the glittering stars
and the likes of me.

Celestia

The next day brings a fresh thought: *Estrella* will understand.
I will tell her what Father said
and she will explain it all away
with her easy laugh and a toss of her head,
pearl bobs dancing at her ears.
I will tell her that I can do without
luxuries and leisure
but I cannot choose to be shunned,
cut off from her,
no longer a member of this family.

People are born with different kinds of courage—
mine is not the courage to be disowned.

Even so, I must say goodbye for now
and on to Europe.
I will entreat her to write every day
with details of the wedding preparations.
Charles is set to arrive tonight for a visit.
I will be on my way to the harbor by then.

∾❀∾

I prepare to knock on Estrella's door
but it is not latched.
It creaks open.

I see only hunched shoulders and a glimpse of skirts
disappearing behind a door across the room.

Mother looks up from the sitting area by the fireplace.
Her eyes are swollen
and a puffy red rash travels around her face and neck,
like continents shifting.
I am moved by her sadness to see me go.
I go to her side to comfort her.

Mimsy turns from the fire,
her wrist draped across the mantel.
She looks at me
but her face remains impassive.
Doors slam.
Servants and maids
flurry and fuss
with trunks and baskets.
My trunk is not among them.

"Take this note to the groundskeeper's office.
Have Mr. Givens dispatch it
to your father at once." Mother presses
a hastily folded slip of her crisp lavender stationery
into my shaking hand.
Mother is still,
compact in her chair,
bobbing on waves of commotion.

"What is happening?" I search their faces.
Mimsy looks away and busies herself with a hatbox.
"We need your father." Mother rotates her handkerchief,
searching for a dry spot. "He must come in from the hunt."
"Is someone ill? Did someone die?"
"Not dead,
yet we shall never see her again." Mother dabs her eyes.

"An unspeakable harm has been done to this family"—
Mimsy narrows her eyes—
"and we need your father's guidance to set it right."
"Though I fear nothing will ever be right again!" says Mother,
shaking into sobs.
Mimsy pats her shoulder.

"Estrella?" I look toward the far door.
Mother can only hold her hand to her mouth and nod.

Estrella's eyes are dark,
her cheeks flushed and splotchy.
She grabs my hands
and pulls me down next to her on the bed.
I see that she is frightened, too,
trying to be brave for me. "Celestia, my angel, you are so dear"—
"What happened?"
"I am afraid that my brilliant future has been abruptly cut short."
"Are you . . . dying?"

"They may act as if I were dead
or worse, as if I were never born,
but you will always know the truth."
"What is it?"
"I trusted the wrong person. That was my undoing."
"Undoing?" I shake my head.

"It was a man. Not Charles. Do you understand what I mean?"
"I think so. . . . No."
"I thought I loved him. Maybe I still do, unworthiness aside."
"So you could just marry him instead."
Estrella drops my hands and turns away.
"Contrary to his every word and deed when we were alone,
he now swears he does not love me,
nor does he consider me an advantageous match."
"But everyone loves you!" I surprise myself by shouting.

"He will not marry me.
He has ruined me
and now will not have me *because* I am ruined"—
she looks into my eyes—
"Do you see, my dear child, how men can do this?
No one tells us this, so I am telling you plainly.
You must be very careful."

"Father will make him marry you! He must!"
"This man is too powerful—
he would destroy *Father* instead.
Besides, now that I see this man

for the loathsome serpent he is,
I would sooner cut out my own heart
than marry him.
Father will send me away.
My things are packed."
Estrella sighs and runs a finger over her bracelets.

"Only for a short while, right?
We will keep it a secret.
You will not be disowned if no one finds out."
"Some secrets do not keep.
It is already done, Celestia.
I am finished . . .
in society . . .
and in this family."
"That cannot be true." Panic rises in my throat, strangling.

"Listen well,
they will say that I am bad,
and try to turn you against me.
But you will remember
that I only made a bad choice,
a mistake,
and when the time came
to pay the price
with my freedom,
I did so willingly
to spare my family.

And you will remember
that I love you always, dearest Celestia."
"I will not let you go!" I cling to her.

She withers and
looks down at her hands
as if they held some answer. "Go now.
My train will not wait."
I cannot stop shaking my head.
"No! No! No!"—more sob than speech.
Mother and Mimsy pull me away.
I am an angry child—
hot helpless tears,
stamping
and struggling.

I do not want to be brave.

✦

Wallpaper roses loom and spin.
Mother's little note is crumpled and damp in my grasp.
Mimsy follows me into the hall,
whispers, "If I can fix this,
I will"—her eyes are wide,
and a bit frightening—
"but I need *time*.
If word gets out,

then it is too late for Estrella."
"Isn't it already too late?
Her bags are packed.
They're sending her away!"

"These are the rules, Celestia:
Your parents must begin the shunning.
If others learn of Estrella's indiscretion,
and she has not been properly disowned,
then our entire family
is ruined,
including your father's business."

"And if she *is* properly disowned . . . ?"
"Damage to the family is . . . tolerable."
Mimsy grimaces. "But Estrella will be lost to us forever.
The limb will be sacrificed
to save the tree, you see."

"But what if others *do not* learn . . . ?"

The corners of Mimsy's mouth twitch
in the beginning of a crafty smile.
"Now you are seeing it my way!
Tell people she has gone abroad,
on holiday,
to act as companion to her withering old auntie!
Tell them anything—
just give me time

to see if I have one last miracle
up my sleeve
before her condition becomes . . .
obvious."

"Do you understand?" Mimsy shakes me a little,
as my mind has gone quite numb,
but I nod.
I need to draw a clear breath
outside.

Thoughts whirl as I descend the stair—
Disowning.
Never speaking Estrella's name.
Never having contact
in person,
or even letters.
Acting as if she were never born.
Severing the limb
before it kills the tree?
I would gladly wear rags
and eat crusts
if I could just keep my sister—
and I rip open the front door.

Wind barrels down the mountain slope
and hits me in the chest.
Air current so swift,
I cannot get a full breath from it.

I run or stumble as best I can,
shoulder against the wind,
across the gray planks of the boardwalk
and up to the stables.

⁙

The tack room air is dark and cool.
It appears very still
save for a tumult of dust in a sliver of sunshine.
I listen for Mr. Givens—
he has one footstep
and one drag,
courtesy of a Rebel cannonball.

"The hunting party is up past the Unger place.
I can't ride in this wind." Givens taps his wooden leg with his
cane.
"I will go."
"You don't know the park. You'll get lost."
"I know it well enough."

His eyes narrow,
he nods to himself,
perhaps recalling a rumor
about one of the guests traipsing about
with the help.

Givens glances toward his horse,
tethered to a post. "Skylark's no tea party pony.
This here's a powerful animal. You ride at all?"

In answer, I jump one foot into the stirrup,
gather my skirts,
and spring up into the saddle.
Skylark skitters slightly
until we get acquainted.
I grab the reins and raise my chin to Givens.
He shrugs and unties the horse.

We take on speed.
Mud spatters everywhere
and my legs are exposed.
The wind carries Givens's voice: "Mind you don't get shot."
We race across the dam
and into the woods.

Peter

Thought I'd seen it all:
sailboats on the mountain,
a debutante gutting a walleye,
but the ground shifts under me
when I see Celestia—

barelegged,
caked in mud—
tearing across the dam on Skylark.

I thought I'd never see her again
after our goodbye,
but now I know
something's changed,
and everything'll be different after this . . .
but how?

Celestia

"Father! Father!"
I shout as I near the bend
so the hunters know to cease shooting.
A lump in my throat interrupts my cry.
I try to shift the lavender paper,
to make out the words,
but wind whips stinging tears from my eyes
and Skylark is moving too fast.

Father does not even know what is wrong yet
but I want desperately to be reassured.
I want him to chuckle
and rest his hand on my head
and say, "It is nothing that cannot be fixed,"

the way he did when I was little,
not like the father who threatened to disown me
just days ago.

The horse bounds up a rocky path now
and I shout when I can get my breath.
Finally the hunting party steps into the path before us.
My father and five other men.
Father looks alarmed
to see me.

"Is anyone ill?" Father squints up at me.
The other men exchange glances
and take a step back.
One epidemic after another has visited in recent years—
diphtheria,
cholera,
tuberculosis.
Any mention of illness
spurs people to flee,
whether it be
ghosts
or contagion itself.

I try to respond
but my throat is tightening uncontrollably.
Father hands his gun to the nearest hunter. "Gentlemen . . ."
I lower myself
and hold the reins out to him.

Father walks me a few paces
away from the men.
He reads the note
and hands it back to me.
"Destroy this," he whispers.

I conceal the paper in my dress waist
while Father mounts Skylark.
His face reveals nothing—
he is already looking ahead
down the trail—
and I follow suit.

Ten eyes stare at me,
perhaps expecting an explanation.
I simply nod
and pick my way
through the rocks and roots
on the craggy path home.
"Miss . . . will you get back okay?" a voice calls.
I just wave.

Later I sneak a look back.
The hunters are blending into the forest,
silent
waves
of greens and browns
in the leaves and branches.

Finally I can retrieve the note:

Estrella ruined!
Come at once!
—Mildred

I tear the note
into the tiniest shreds possible,
planning to sink it
to the bottom of the lake
forever.

Peter

I row toward the dam—
my only chance to see Celestia again.
But it's her father
who thunders past on horseback.
That means Celestia'll be on foot.

I turn the boat in just past Sheep's Head Point,
one of our meeting places.
I make the birdcall,
ruffed grouse,
but she's already waiting there
in the shadows
between a rock and the underbrush.

Just as I start out of the boat to tie it up,
Celestia gets in.
"My family needs me."
I help her get settled and begin to row.
"What's wrong?"
"You can never tell anyone . . ."
"I swear."
"My sister is . . . ruined.
They are sending her away.
Disowning her."
Celestia leans forward,
peering toward the clubhouse.

We reach the middle of the lake
in time to see a carriage dart out
from behind the clubhouse
and tear for the main road,
bumping across the dam too fast.

Celestia jumps to her feet.
The little boat rocks
and I reach for her hand.
We watch the carriage take the last turn
on two wheels
and right itself
safely
as our boat capsizes.

The last thing we see
before we go under
is clots of mud flying
as the carriage disappears
down the hill.

❧

We're strong swimmers,
both of us,
but I don't let go of her hand
just the same.
When we surface
and the lake water has streamed off our faces,
she says, "That would have been my carriage.
Mimsy is taking *Estrella* abroad instead."

I can't help a selfish thought. "I'm not sorry
that it isn't you in the carriage.
Maybe we'll have a few more days."
"Let's meet tonight"—she smiles a little—
"I'll try to get away."
But her lips are bluing already
and the wind's too strong to be long in the water.
We heave ourselves into the boat
and I row us to the dock,
even though someone might see us—
what choice do we have?

"Do you want me to come with you?"
I look toward the clubhouse,
which we've never entered together.
She squares her shoulders
and shakes her head.
I let her go.

Celestia

The foyer is very still compared to the wind.
Voices drift from the game room:
Mrs. Godwin and Mrs. Marshall.
"I could swear I saw spots—"
"Such a shame."
"—and on that beautiful face."
"Such a complexion—of course it will be ruined."
"If she even lives."
I let the screen door bang behind me, and the voices stop.
I sense them waiting,
so I step into view,
water running off me in sheets.
Are they gossiping about Estrella?
About her abrupt departure?
I feel the need to stare them down.
They harrumph and return to their card game.
I head for the stairs,
leaving behind a puddle on the floor.

"Insolent girl!"
one whispers,
but loud enough for me to hear.
"I declare, I've never seen one bolder."
"And soaking wet!"
"That child *always* seems to be dripping!"

I climb the stairs
lead-legged
and wet-heavy.

How quickly tall tales begin—
Estrella is spirited away
and these windbags
have her dying of some plague or another.
Better that they are off the trail
of the truth, I suppose.
One thing for sure,
the whole clubhouse will be buzzing
about epidemics
through the afternoon
and most of dinner.

I return to the last place I saw my family.
The door is ajar.
Estrella's sitting room is laid bare.
No sign that she ever inhabited this place

or that she even existed,
save one length of scarlet embroidery thread
curled up on the settee.

The chill has my bones now
and I shudder.
Is this how it feels to be disowned?
Out in the cold,
shunned from the warmth of the hearth?

I dash down the main corridor
to my parents' suite.
Their hall door is locked.
They are speaking low
and I press my ear to the door.

❧

"How long has this been going on?" Father's heavy footfall
suggests he is pacing the floor.
"I do not know."
"Well, how long have *you* known?"
"She herself did not know
the fact of her condition
until recent days." Mother's voice is high and thin.
"That is it, then—she is cut off!
Disowned!
Disinherited!"

"Where did we go wrong?" Mother sobs.
"She is dead to us. Let me never hear her name again."
"Lower your voice. Please, calm down."
"And the other one—
her sister—
is not far behind her!" Father bangs something,
glasses rattle. "We must get *her* settled
in an advantageous match
while we still have bargaining power."

"Another problem, what about Charles?"—
Mother's voice rises—
"He is on his way here
this very minute."
"Well then, Estrella can *marry* him. Quickly!
Before her figure swells like a dirigible!"—
Father's tone brightens—
"We'll have a wedding
instead of a disaster."
"No, it is too late.
He will see with his own eyes before long.
And what incentive would he have
not to leave her flat once he realizes?"

Father sounds as if his teeth are clenched:
"Then we must force the hand
of the one responsible,
make *his* family feel the threat of this shame."

"Good, whatever it takes to keep our daughter."

"Who is he?
That moon-eyed fop always at her elbow?
Blond fellow?"—Father speaks quickly—
"A good bit fancier than I would have pictured for a son-in-law,
but beggars cannot be choosers."
"That choosing has already passed, but—" Mother tries to interject.

"What is his name again?" Father must be shuffling papers.
Mother hurries to get the words out: "You are thinking
of young Frederick, but—"
"I will *make* it happen. I could shut down
Fred Senior's whole Pittsburgh operation
with one stroke of a pen, and everyone knows it."

Mother's voice strains slightly: "Bertram, darling!"
"Hmm?"
"Frederick is not the one."
"No? Then . . . who?"
My mother utters a sound so low,
I cannot make out the name.
A chair scratches against the floor.

"Grayson? That lecher!"
"Hush! Bertram!"
"For the love of God, Mildred,
what was she thinking?"
A pounding comes next,

like a fist on a table,
and something smashes.
"Thinking did not rule the day, apparently." Mother sniffs.

My father's whisper is hoarse,
as if the air has all gone out of him:
"He can destroy us, Mildred.
Everything we have built.
We have no recourse
against a man like that."
"But, Bertram—"
"Mildred . . . you know what we have to do."
Mother's response is a fresh wave of sobs.

Apparently, she knows the rules of shunning
as well as Mimsy:
they will deny Estrella's existence
to protect the family
and its position in society.
How could they do this?
Are money
and rich friends
more important
than their daughter?

Or daughters.

I imagine myself lying across the threshold
waiting to be found,

to be comforted
like an old dog.
Huddled with my arms around my knees,
I give in to loss and frustration,
to consuming grief.
Hot tears soak through my cold, wet dress.
My sobs turn to shivers.
I suddenly feel so tired.
My head rests on the warm dark door.

I must stop this somehow . . .
by helping Mimsy . . .
by preventing
the disowning from becoming public,
or worse,
the suspicions regarding Estrella's virtue
from becoming fodder
for nosy society crones.

I must save my sister.

A warm towel,
dry clothes,
eyes cried empty and swollen,
I cannot stop myself from crawling under the covers
and succumbing to sleep, however fitful.

When I rise from the overheated nap,
it is already dark
and my stomach tells me I missed tea
and maybe dinner.
Yawning, I start for the stairs,
toward the smell of roast chicken,
creamed pearl onions,
maybe a fruit pie. . . .
The heavy door of the front room opens
and Charles exits in a band of light.
Estrella's fiancé!

It all rushes back to me:
I might never see my sister again.
I stifle a gasp.
I want to hear what Charles is saying.

"I should have known
it was too good to be true." His thin shoulders slump
more than usual.
A low voice responds from inside the room.
I recognize the cadence of my father's speech.
The light goes out.

Father exits,
closing the door behind him.
The two men are shadows

amid the moonlight's reflection
off polished wood.

"That's just how women are—changeable,
like the weather," Father says.
Charles nods
and coughs, then says, "I was a fool
to think someone like Estrella
could ever grow to love me."
"Your father and I will work out the details
of terminating the arrangement
in a way that avoids any embarrassment
for your family."
They shake hands.
"Good luck to you, son."
Charles does not look back.

The wedding is off.
A whole lifetime of plans
swallowed up by the night in a matter of seconds.

Father, ever the businessman,
has let Charles go
before he could quit,
before word
of Estrella's predicament
could reach his ears.

There is more haste than usual in Charles's departure.
Horses whinny and buck,
raising a great clatter as the carriage starts for town.
I imagine Charles mortified at the commotion,
dabbing his hankie at his brow
and the corners of his mouth.

Interior doors slam,
hall doors open,
lighting the corridor behind me.
Faces appear in the doorways,
looking up and down the hall.
Mrs. Godwin holds up her lamp to see my face,
then scowls
and slams her door.
A child's voice from another door: "Is it the fever?"
A stern voice from inside: "Come away from the door!
If you catch it,
we'll all be dead by Sunday."

I turn back to Father,
but the front room door is closing
on his trail of cigar smoke.
A band of light appears beneath the door.
I tiptoe down the stairs

and toward the back door
to head for the staff cabins.

⟡

Words float back to me:
spots,
beautiful face,
complexion,
ruined,
fever.
Rumors have already started,
but not the right one,
thank goodness.
Unless someone *else* is ill . . .

Peter is already waiting.
He meets me halfway
on the path.
We duck into the trees,
always conscious of being seen.

I want to pour the whole mess out to him
but I am afraid it is too awful.
I cannot form my mouth around the words anyway
before he says,
"It's gone all through the staff cabins like wildfire."
"The fever?"
"The rumor."

Peter still holds my arm.
It is very dark.
Perhaps I could not ask it
if I could see his face more clearly
or if he could see mine:
"What are they saying?"

"It could be just talk
and, keep in mind,
by foolish girls, some of them,
scullery maid and the char girl especially . . ."
"Yes, yes, go on." I need to know if it is the truth
they are spreading,
or speculation.
". . . and they might be jealous of your sister
because of her looks
and having so many fancy things to wear—"
I grab his shoulders. "Say it!"
"They say Estrella is . . . expecting."

"They say your sister's soiled goods
and now no dandy
or son of a steel man
will have her." Peter gently takes my hands
from his shoulders.

The staff!
They know!
And, first thing in the morning,
they will tell the servants in the clubhouse
who come with the families.
Then those servants will whisper it to their employers.

Peter puts an arm around me as we walk.
"To the staff, it's still just a rumor.
Estrella's gone.
They can't prove it."
I nod. "Rumors are just as often false,
are they not?
Though her sudden retreat
might incriminate . . .
Oh, Peter, how can I make
every nosy old busybody
forget about Estrella?"

"Well, I'll tell you,
by sunrise tomorrow,
every serving girl
is gonna bring this news
up those stairs with the breakfast tray"—
Peter steers me by the elbow—
"so you'd better think of something tonight."

"I wish I could make them all go away."

. . . If you catch it, we'll all be dead by Sunday.

By the time we reach the lantern light
of the clubhouse porch,
I know what to do.
The perfect distraction.
A way to make everyone scatter,
or at least lock themselves in their rooms.
Even the scandal-seeking vultures
will remove themselves from society with others.

Club members will be so consumed
with concern for themselves
and their own families,
suspicions about Estrella
will disperse
like fog off the lake.

"Peter, I know how to keep the truth a secret."
"What can I do to help?"
I think for a moment. "Berries.
Pick some.
Or get preserves from the pantry.
Anything red.
Then meet me back here."
Peter pauses. "What else?"
I take a deep breath. "A kiss for luck?"

Even before the kiss
my heart is beating so hard
that it scarcely leaves room for air.

Peter bolts
and I take off at a dead run
for the dam.

When I return,
Peter joins me on the road
just before the clubhouse.
I catch my breath
and place his hand on my face.
"How do I feel?"
"Damp?"
"Would you say 'clammy'?"
"Maybe."
"Hot?"
Peter starts to nod,
a look of understanding spreads across his face.
He holds up the berries in his handkerchief.
"You really think you can get away with this?"
"This will never work, right?"
"I don't know. How good an actress are you?"
"Mmm." I shake my head. "I must *try*, at least."
I watch him carefully squeeze some berry juice
onto his palm.
When I reach for his hand,
he holds it away. "They'll see the stain on your fingers."
"Right. Mind my dress then, too."

He dabs my cheeks.
"Hurry, I'm beginning to cool."
He kisses my nose. "You smell delicious."
"Do you think they'll notice?"
He shrugs and wipes his hands on his handkerchief.

Our walk to the porch
is solemn;
our kiss too quick.

I stretch out on the porch floor. "Ring the bell.
And run."
Peter rings the old ship's bell over and over,
then darts into the shadows.

The door opens and I pretend to moan.

A voice says, "What's this?"
then yells back into the clubhouse: "Get Mr. Whitcomb!"

Footsteps,
and the voice comes closer. "What happened to you?"
A hand pushes the hair from my face.
A gasp . . .
"Fever?"
Footsteps again.
And the bell ringing.

The voice cries, "Fever is here!
Scarlet fever!"

⌒☙❦❧⌒

Bustling begins immediately.
I hear movement throughout the clubhouse
and an errand boy yelling "Fever!"
as he runs to the guest cottages.

I hear the clicking of little-dog nails
on the wooden porch floor.
That mongrel sniffs my cheeks,
getting ready for a lick, no doubt.

Father arrives. "My God, Celestia!"—
feels my forehead—"you're burning up!"
His arms go under my shoulders and knees.
He grunts as he stands.
I let my free arm and neck go limp.

The voice says, "You can't bring her in here!
It is contagious!"

"Stand aside, Louise,
or I'll run you over." Father is turning
to get us through the door.
I squint through my lashes.

Mrs. Godwin harrumphs,
and her little dog yelps
when she backs up and
steps on him.

From my window
I can see by moonlight
Mrs. Godwin handing an ornate birdcage into her carriage.
Her coat is over a dressing gown,
her hair still set in rags.

Others wait anxiously for the carriages to return,
sitting on steamer trunks
or hastily tied bundles of whatever
they think they cannot live without—
absurd
rich refugees.

I cannot believe my plan is working—
everyone is leaving.

Their grumbling floats up to my ears:
". . . not the season for scarlet fever . . ."
". . . cannot quarantine everybody . . ."
". . . take her all the way to Pittsburgh in the carriage . . . ?"
". . . private train car . . . ?"

Mother is frantic,
entreating Father to hurry in packing,
debating burning our clothes and bedding,
fretting about the haste of the drivers,
checking my forehead
every few minutes
while I will myself
to remain hot.
The lights are low
so I splash my cheeks quickly
when Mother leaves the room.
I cannot risk the smell of strawberries
riding in the carriage with us
all the way to Pittsburgh.
Mother returns
and pronounces me "cooler, but quite damp."

I feel the unease of my secret.

I want to talk it over with Peter before we leave,
but our carriage is ready
and Mother would never let me out of her sight.
She clings
as Father carries me
and hurries us down the hall
as if we could stay one step ahead of death.

What have I done?
It is all happening so fast.
Surely I did not think it through.

The bags are stowed.
Father settles me in the carriage
and goes to help Mother.
I sneak a look around.
Peter is just out of reach
in the shadows
by the treeline.
No last kiss?
No last embrace?
I did not consider this consequence.
Surely he is thinking the same thing.
Surely he understands.

Father climbs in after Mother. "Driver!"
The carriage lurches forward.

So this is the final goodbye,
this artless parting,
until next season.

I watch Peter until my eyes sting.
He does not wave.

So much can change in a year.

OFF-SEASON

1888–1889

Nursing School

Kate

Student nurses' house:
sign in,
choose a bed,
no window—
less draft.
Others might care for a view,
but not this girl.
Keeping the body functioning—
that's the job.
That's what we're here to learn.

Suitcase under bed.
Long room,

empty and silent.
Dusty yellow light
lies in squares.
Camphor,
gauze,
and
cod liver oil
the only perfume,
except perhaps
the iron smell
of bed frames
and laundry starch.

Pure physical order.
Lungs breathe at last.
Hear footsteps clicking in the hall.
Breath hesitates.
Sitting resumes.
Not waiting.
Just existing.

Nursing shifts are long.
Clock turns twice
with scant hours of sleep.
No breaks.
Training is doing.

Stop the wound.
Catch the blood,
or the sick.
The sights,
the smells—
new girls turn away
pale
or faint
or retch.
Or they fall
exhausted.
I take over their shifts.

Student house is gone cold
for holiday break.
Winter blows through
empty halls.
Mud's frozen solid.
No meals.
No one knows
I remain.

Set by a secret store
of food,
but mice got in.
Throw it all away.
Filthy varmints.

Pile up blankets
from other girls' beds.
Stay under there, mostly,
all day.

⁓᯼⁓

Alone in the student house,
starving,
cold,
and stubborn,
I don't mean to hear church bells
on Christmas Day.
Bundle up,
go out
to track the sound
and find the church they belong to.
Follow the priest
to the little side house.

Hide behind a tree
until he's gone,
then ring for the housekeeper
at the back door.

We strike a deal.
She's happy enough
to get free
of the heavy work,

and I get a bellyful
of roast duck
and mince pie—
yes,
before I can stop myself,
mince pie.

Nearly black out
from nourishment.

Nursing staff graduates me quick,
gives the address
of the New York doctor
who will employ me.
No sense wishing for home
or what might have been.

Head Nurse and the others
are glad to be rid of me,
they make no secret of it.
They raise eyebrows,
shake heads
when they see
I can't stop polishing
and counting instruments,
counting boxes of supplies,
counting chairs,

people,
windowpanes,
tiles . . .
Even sitting still and silent—
the teachers can surely tell—
I'm counting.

East Conemaugh

Maura

Nights in this valley can be long and cold,
especially for the wife of a railroad man,
so I bring my basket of scraps near the fire
to start a new quilt.
It warms me as I work
and sets me to remembering
my own girlhood
on a little farm in these hills:
a little plot of soil
for potatoes and beans,
a chicken coop,
a pig, a horse, sometimes a cow,
a tiny slant-roof house,

and all five kids burrowing under the blankets
as the fire died down.

My little ones sigh in their beds,
the one yet-to-be turns in my belly—
this quilt will be for them,
to tell them the story of my life,
and how it began their lives.

The dampness
in this valley
is a constant companion,
at least until Joseph gets home.
I toss on another log
and it burns colors.
I begin my quilt
with a faded blue like violets
cut into a little slant house.

Ears straining for the engine whistle,
resting my feet on a stone warmed by the fire,
I smooth Joseph's panel
over my lap:
a copper-haired baby taking his first steps
on a gray-brown ship,
leaving behind the green green hills
of Ireland.

The copper scrap is cut
from the last short dress of my girlhood.
His ship is a leftover from making
new thick wool work pants.
And the still-fresh green
is from my old dress sleeves—
when the elbows wore out,
the dress became a skirt.
I stitch these pictures to solid squares,
alternate them
with simple pieced
nine-patch squares.

The squares of our youth—
my little blue slant house,
his green hills still warm with sunshine—
connect to
the center panel of our union.
This is our family tree.

I work the last stitches
on the middle square:
mountain laurel
in bloom
like the June bride
that I was,
white lace
and blushing
ever so slightly pink.

I am about to roll the stone
toward the fire one more time
when I hear my husband's special signal just for me:
one long pull, then two short.
I sing along, *tooooooooooot-toot-toot*,
through smiling lips.

I pack my piecework into the basket
with a humming and tapping of foot,
put the fire to bed
and pull the pins from my hair.
I rub knuckles to cheeks
and race to the door,
his blushing bride once again.

Joseph walks toward the house
in that slow way,
grinning. "There's my bright-eyed girl!"
He lifts me into his arms.
"Careful. The baby."
We both look down at my belly
and laugh at the wonder of it.

I free the buttons on his work shirt
and he closes the door
on the blessedly long, long winter night.

South Fork Fishing and Hunting Club
Lake Conemaugh

Peter

Dear Celestia,

Winter on the lake.
I wish you could see it
and hear the quiet of the snowfall.

Only a few of us up here.
A skeleton crew.
The cabins are so God-awful cold
and the larder's full of mice.

I read your letters every night,
until I fall asleep.

I found some old snowshoes
in the clubhouse
and asked around if I could use them.
One fella said they belong to old peg-leg Givens
and he won't be needing them,
or at least one of them.

Well, we had quite a laugh,
but later I felt bad about it.
I wondered if Givens has the
phantom pain
you hear about,
an ache where a piece of him used to be,
and I got to feeling pretty bad for old Givens,
because that's how I feel
without you.

Is he missing that old leg?
Wondering if it's moving on
to have a great life
without him?
Is it thinking of him? (Ha-ha.)

I guess Papa's probably right—
what could possibly come of this?
Maybe we don't have to know.

I just know I keep feeling this way,
wishing you were near,
wishing it was summer
all year
forever.

Truly yours,
Peter

Institut Villa Mont Choisi
Switzerland

Celestia

Directrice Blanchard confiscates Peter's letters—
Father paid her handsomely for her trouble, I am sure—
so I intercept the letter carrier at the corner.

Every day the mailman on the corner.
Every day the envelope with the small scratchy lettering.
Every day bliss in my hand.

One day in March the letters stop.

One letter that had no trouble getting through:

Daughter:

Your mother and I have arranged for a suitable match—
A suitable match!
—and plans will progress immediately upon your return.
First, your coming-out cotillion:
time is of the essence, so
we may not wait for the social season,
but instead will proceed with
a small, tasteful
coming-out party
hosted by your aunt.
Then expect a proper engagement with announcements
and a ball in honor of your betrothed
to be given by your mother and me
as soon as propriety permits—
Oh, dread! Who can it be?
I skip ahead through all the parts
about persevering in my studies
and how "delicate" my health has been
since that "sudden brief fever"
at the club last year.
I try not to revisit
the long night in the carriage,

my inexplicably quick recovery,
and the interminable weeks confined to bed anyway.
You will be under strict supervision this summer.
Cavorting with unseemly acquaintances,
thus jeopardizing your health
and your good standing in society,
will not be tolerated.
Mother will escort you to meals
and one hour of bathing in the lake daily . . .
etc.
etc.
etc.
Oh, by the way, the chap is Andrew Forrester—
That dullard!
Your mother says he looks quite dashing in his jodhpurs.
He has been all over the world big-game hunting, you know—
I know. I know!
He cannot help but remind one,
seemingly with every breath.
Always posing
with his dusty stuffed animal heads.
Reliving some tiresome story
of stalking through the jungle,
or stalking through the savannah . . .
always ending with *POW!*
and pretending to shoot something.
—Forresters are an impeccable family. Could not ask for better.
And they are equally pleased with the alignment.
I know you will do right by this family!

And *I know* that he wants me married off quickly—
in the event that Estrella's secret gets out,
I will already be "settled."
Mere suspicion can be damaging enough,
and no one in society
would consider aligning
with a family disgraced.

⤶ ❧ ⤷

In the crosshairs of an arranged marriage,
I continue to write to Peter every day,
hoping his feelings have not changed.
But *I* have changed:
I already knew he was the one for me,
but now,
in this silence . . .
I realize I cannot endure
a life without his love.

Wild with imaginings,
I spend my last days in Switzerland
gripping the balusters of my balcony,
searching the gray sky for answers.
Is he thinking of me?
Does he feel the same as before?

Not knowing
is actually worse

than bad news.
Not knowing
has shaken me,
until all other fear
falls loose.

PRE-SUMMER SEASON

1889

En Route to the Allegheny Mountains

Celestia

Father comes alone
to fetch me at the harbor.
He hands me
my embroidered bag,
which Mother has filled
with a few summer things
and a lavender note saying
that we will all be together soon.
Not all! Not Estrella—I clench my teeth
and crumple the lie in my fist—
and not her baby.

Of course Estrella cannot write
to tell us about the child—
or if she did, Father would burn the letters
privately, secretly,
as our society dictates—
but I pray that
both are alive and well.
Will I ever know?

We take the train directly to South Fork
without first going home to Pittsburgh.
A bit ahead of the resort season,
we will wait there alone
for Mother—and other club members—
to join us.

"We are going to have a quiet summer, young lady."
Father, holding a big black umbrella,
hands me into the carriage at South Fork station.
"None of that nonsense like last year."
"Yes, Father," I shout over the din of rain.
He climbs in and shuts the door,
whisking rain off his sleeves.
"I should have had that boy fired.
I sent word last month, but they assure me
he is no longer in their employ."
"Oh?" I try not to look too interested.
The whip cracks;
the carriage jolts forward.

Father turns his attention back to his papers,
but quickly succumbs
to the rocking motion
and nods off.
I remove a passel of envelopes
from the lining of my jacket.

My fingers instinctively find my favorite
letter from Peter
and I read it again,
even though I can recite every word.

Dear Celestia,

Remember my favorite fishing hole?
That's where I first saw you.
It's all covered with snow now,
but I pretend you're there,
reading a book in the sun,
and you can hear me.
I tell you everything,
starting with how much I miss you. . . .

⁓⋇⁓

The incessant rain on the roof
of the carriage
is deafening.
The threat of a wheel loosening

or sticking in mud,
or a washout on the road
prevents sleep from coming.
We creep toward Lake Conemaugh.

I long for the featherbed,
a hot bath poured with steaming kettles,
and perhaps a game hen or quail
with early potatoes and fennel.
But the season has not yet begun
and most staff are not in residence.
What could be my last night
of luxury
will likely include
a musty room in need of airing,
a bowl of tepid water,
and a dusty biscuit with salt pork.

Father snores
through the interminable racket.
He does not suspect that tomorrow
I will risk losing him
and the comfortable life I know.

Tomorrow I set off to find Peter.

South Fork Fishing and Hunting Club
Lake Conemaugh

Celestia

We arrive well past midnight.
Givens waits with an umbrella
to escort us through the mud
to the clubhouse.
Father offers to carry me across
to save my new shoes—
kidskin,
soft as gloves,
with beadwork
and satin ribbon,
fresh from Paris.

I consider these shoes
and what kind of life
they would carry a girl into.
A chateau or villa
with gardens
in the summer, and
in winter
a house in town
with parties
and a deep soft chair
by the fire,
with walls and walls of books,
children snuggling in and
demanding bedtime stories,
tea in fine china cups.
A perfectly lovely life
in many ways,
but I cannot conjure up the man
who fits in that picture—
husband,
father for those children,
reader by the fire. . . .

I would rather have no husband
than the wrong husband.

I pull on my overshoes
and splash my own way
to the steps.

When Givens and his crew bring up the bags,
I corner the young stable hand.
He says that Peter received word from the valley
that he was needed
at home.

I sneak down to the pantry
for whatever I can stash in my pockets.
I have a little money in my purse.

I look in on my father sleeping
and say a silent goodbye.
Perhaps I will be back before dinnertime,
before Father even notices I am gone,
if Peter has truly cast me aside.
But then, perhaps
it is goodbye forever.

Johnstown

Peter

So tired.
The stove's gone out again
and the ceiling's dripping in one corner.
I can't seem to raise myself.

When will this hell of rain end?
I haven't seen the stars in so long.

Conemaugh Valley

Celestia

In Peter's world
I will not have carriages,
so I walk.

Instantly drenched
and cold
in the predawn fog,
I am relieved to reach South Fork,
where South Fork Creek meets the Little Conemaugh,
and board the train.

The sky is white
and the rivers reflect it,

surging over their banks
and through the woods,
trees black and shining wet.

On any day,
just before dawn,
the world is black and white
like a photograph
and the colors come gradually.
But today they never come.

I feel entirely unreal—
like this colorless world
must be the view through a stereopticon,
and I have gone to live in its images.
When I close my eyes,
and open them again,
I will surely be snug and dry
in my bed by the window,
watching the mist lift off Lake Conemaugh,
safe in the embrace of my family,
not this specter
without form
or mass.

But I know I am flesh
because a shiver passes through.
My sodden dress

is dripping
on the floor of the train car.
A tiny rivulet
runs across the aisle
and a dry lady there
scowls at me
and lifts her feet.
Her shoes are immaculate.

The train creeps over a viaduct,
high over the roiling water below.
We pass the rows of white houses
on the flats of Mineral Point,
then on to East Conemaugh.
There I see a girl my age
sweeping the threshold of her house
across from the train yard.

She looks serene,
resting her chin on her broom handle.
Perhaps all her questions are answered already.

A toddler pushes past her,
then another,
then another,
upending a pot of red geraniums.

They chase rings around her
and stretch arms up.
She leans down
and hugs and teases,
then shepherds them back into the house.

Her face looks older to me now
as she scans the sky
and the hills
before closing the door.

My stomach is fairly insistent
that I stop for refreshment.
The bit of bread is gone
and I forgo the apple—
an apple on an empty stomach
only aggravates one's hunger.

The tendrils of smoke appear on the horizon,
then the smokestacks
and taller buildings.
Johnstown is all before us.
Mills,
factories,
churches,
offices,
stores,

homes,

not altogether different from Pittsburgh.

Industry,

progress,

and, I hope, a good strong cup of tea.

Johnstown

Celestia

The waiter girl
brings scones and cream
and a second cup of tea.
I hand her the envelope
from one of Peter's letters
and she points the way to his street.

I give her the coins for my meal
and an extra for herself.
She looks pleased
and pockets her gratuity.

How will I survive if I stay in Johnstown?
Will I have the price of a cup of tea in my purse?
Will *I* be the waiter girl next time?

I picture Estrella in the cheap muslin apron,
pouring tea for strangers
in a foreign land.
Or serving as companion and assistant
to an old widow
low on the social scale
who takes her in
in lieu of a salary.
Or maybe using her sewing skill
to make hats for a milliner.
She might glean some small joy from that.

These are the fates
of disowned daughters—
you hear of them
in only the faintest whispers—
the most they can hope for.
These are my fates now.

Finally I stand before Peter's house:
a small
white
square

frame house,
a bit of fence in front.
Perhaps I stand too long.
A door slams
and a neighbor woman glares. "You have business here?"
Her hair is crinkly gray
and her skin is grayer.
"I am a friend . . ." I nod toward Peter's home.
"Well, a friend is what they're needing, that's for sure."
"Oh?"
"Hard times"—she nods her gray head—
"I been helping what I could,
but I got my own houseful."
"I am sure they are grateful," I say, not sure at all.
Not sure of anything.
"Well, you best get to it, then." The woman jabs a thumb
in the direction of Peter's house,
and I take those last steps
into my new life.

⚜

A garden grew here once,
a tiny parterre
in the square that would be a yard.
The center has something
that was once a sundial,
stone
and iron.

Flower boxes overflow with weeds.
A woman lived here once,
but a long time ago.

I knock. Knock again.
The only answer is coughing.

Fear of imposing
is overtaken by concern
and I try the door.

My eyes adjust to the dimness.
The air is damp
and smells of sickness.
Coughing
and moaning
come from the bedroom straight ahead,
punctuated by dripping
in the open doorway.
Someone in the bed.

"Peter?"
It takes an eternity
to cross the main room.
"Peter?"
The face is not his.
An older man,
subtly familiar.
Peter's father.

He squints at me. "Anna?"
He becomes agitated.
"You've come for me at last.
Where have you been so long?"
Ashen,
eyes enormous,
he tries to raise himself,
tangling in the bedding.

"Please, sir . . . I am Peter's friend . . ."
Too frightened to finish,
I back away
and run aground
something,
ricochet into the doorjamb.
"Peter!"

How glad I am to see him!
Even slouching
under a blanket,
red-eyed,
unshaven.
He wavers.
I reach out to steady him.

He looks at me blankly
at first,
perhaps not understanding
how I had come to be there,

then raises his arms.
The blanket becomes wings.
He is broader
but thinner.
My arms go round
ribs.
My head does not rest
on the smooth rise of his chest
as it once did,
but on collarbones.

His woolen embrace
envelopes me, though,
and I feel warm for the first time today.

He leans on me,
too hard.
His eyes wander to the ceiling.
"Peter, what is wrong?"
I help him to a plank chair
near the potbelly stove, expecting heat
but finding the metal grate cold.
"So tired," he sighs. "I'm just so tired."

⤳✻⤳

Once the stove is going,
I rearrange the blankets
and tuck him into a cot by the door.

The rocker in the corner
yields a cushion
and I stuff it under his head.
At last, the dark chill
is off the room.

I search for food
in the cupboard,
anything to give them
before I go.

I count the coins in my purse,
cover my head with Peter's coat,
and run for the shops,
hoping for a baker,
some soup vegetables,
and strong coffee.

Bread,
broth,
and kindness,
a cool hand on the brow,
this is all I know to do.
I stoke the fire,
rock in the chair
under Peter's coat,

and listen to the rain
and the rivers.

I recall the sound of
South Fork Creek cascading
from the spillway
higher up on the mountain,
and imagine that same water
rushing by me now in Johnstown
by way of the Little Conemaugh.
Then that river joins the Stony Creek
roaring into Johnstown from the south.
Three rivers . . .
all overflowing their banks,
creeping up like a tide . . .

Sleep slips over me like a veil.
I dream a woman is watching me,
eyes earnest,
a sympathetic turn to her mouth,
but
I must be awake
and it is only a portrait of Peter's mother
above the stove.
This must be Anna,
I hear my own thought
as I give in to sleep.

Peter

Gone down under the waves now.
Exhaustion's claimed me.
I dreamed of Celestia,
that she was
right here in the house,
tending Papa and me
like an angel.

I had no choice
but to quit
the vigil
I've been keeping
at his bedside;
sleep crushed me.

I wish so bad
she was really here.

South Fork Fishing and Hunting Club
Lake Conemaugh

Whitcomb

Making headway on a stack of contracts,
I notice
unease
tugging at my sleeve.
I neaten up the papers,
open my ledger,
close it again.
What is this irritation
at the edge of my thoughts?
Damn these intrusions!
Time wasters!

I have no choice
but to push my work away
for the moment
and clear my head.

It is Celestia.
She did not appear for breakfast—
not unusual—
a busy man such as myself
often begins his workday
before other members of the household
are even awake.
But now it is well past eleven
and I have not yet heard her stirring
or seen her traipsing
down the stairs with a book in hand.

Perhaps the trip exhausted her.
I head upstairs and knock on her door.
No answer.
A quick look in her room
reveals she must be up and about.

Not in the clubhouse.
I look out the windows
to see rain pelting the boardwalks
and whipping the lake.
She could not be out there . . .
could she?

I grab a mackintosh to hold over my head
and go out
toward the stables.
I am forced to yell over the sound of the rain:
"Has anybody seen my daughter today?"
Givens shakes his head. "Sorry, Mr. Whitcomb."
"Off somewhere with her nose in a book, no doubt," I say.
No need to raise suspicions
among the staff . . .
though I cannot help but glance toward the dam
and the valley below.

⁕

Nightfall.
No sign of Celestia.
I pace the bedroom floor
in my dressing gown,
chewing a cigar.
Oh, how Mildred would protest
if she were here.

I open the door to
look down the empty hall,
or stop to listen,
my ears perked up
like a deer in these woods
fearing us hunters,
but the only sound is rain.

"Where did I leave those matches?"
As I reach for them on the mantel
my sleeve brushes the hinged double frame:
portraits of the girls.
The first frame,
Estrella's place,
is empty.
The second is Celestia,
all in white,
with flowers in her hair
instead of fancy jewels—
not like other girls.
Her mother's eyes,
my set jaw—
she has a look of certainty,
as if she knows exactly who she is.
I find myself wishing
for the hundredth time that night
that *I* knew exactly who she was.

"Celestia?" I call in a normal voice
as if expecting her to answer,
as if it were any old night.

But the silence,
the finality,
gnaws around my edges,
until I am thoroughly frightened.
"Celestia!" I yell,

hating the trembling in my voice.
This time I know there will be no answer.

My legs give way
without permission
and I am on the floor.

All my money,
all my influence and connections
can provide no remedy.
Look at yourself, Bertram,
reduced to this—
a heap on the floor,
a weeping man in his dressing gown
whispering to his daughter's image,
"Celestia, my sensible girl,
I cannot lose another daughter
to romantic foolishness."

Johnstown

Celestia

Peter sleeps peacefully now.
After mumbling and tossing at first,
he went still under the heaviness
of desperate sleep.
I rock myself in his mother's chair.
When I open my eyes
to the early light,
Peter is staring at me.

I sit up, surprised.
"How long have you been awake?" I ask,
hoping his answer will prove him to be lucid.
His voice is unsteady: "This must be heaven, right?

I thought it would look different.
Clouds at least.
How else could you be here,
sleeping in my sitting room?"
"Railroads.
And one very large ship."

He raises one arm,
sinewy,
veined.
I go to him,
hold his hand.

"I'm glad you're here"—he looks around—
"I thought I was dreaming."
"Your letters stopped. I just had to know . . ."
"Working double shifts to pay for doctors.
Up with him most of the night,
thinking every cough'll kill him . . .
black lung,
the miner's death.
And me, I'm just exhausted."
"I understood as soon as I arrived." I smooth the blankets.
"I'm sorry"—his hands stop mine—"I should have let you know."
I sit beside him. "Now I know it was only the letters that stopped."
Peter holds my hands to his chest. "My intentions
have not changed.
And you . . .
feel the same?

Since you *are* here?"
"Yes." I smile and he sinks back into the pillows.

He sits up again. "Well, how *can* you be here—
do your parents know?
Are they alive?
They must've been lost at sea!"
"They made an arrangement—
a choice that would force me into a life
that I would find intolerable." I look away.
He gently guides my chin
until our eyes meet again. "A match?"
"To a half-wit braggart."
"Celestia!"
"I had to escape it and I had to find you
before you lost your love for me."
Peter kisses my hands. "That'll never happen."

South Fork Fishing and Hunting Club
Lake Conemaugh

Whitcomb

Givens limps into the front room.
"Raining buckets again today, sir."
I draft letters
at the big mahogany desk in the front room.
"I am aware of that, Mr. Givens."
"Your girl'd be sore afraid
lost in the woods
on a day like this, sir."
"I am sure she would"—I keep my eyes trained on
my papers—"if she were, in fact, lost."
"If you'd be wanting me to send to South Fork
for a search party,

we could maybe find her
before nightfall."

I take a deep breath
and place my pen precisely
in the center of my book
before looking up. "Thank you, Mr. Givens,
that is not necessary."
"Well, now, I know she's got spunk and all, but . . ."
"She is not lost in the woods"—I push my chair back
and rise,
looking out the window
in the direction of the valley—"and I am almost certain
that she does not wish to be found."
Givens joins me by the window and nods. "Aye,
the boy from the valley . . ."
I am taken aback,
as always,
by how much the help know
of our personal affairs.
I resume my seat
and take up my papers. "Shut the door behind you, Givens.
I am not to be disturbed again."

I extract a fresh sheet of stationery.
No point in delaying;
it cannot be avoided any longer.

Dearest Mildred,

Celestia is missing.
I believe she has left us for the Johnstown boy.
I will confirm this, then join you at home.
Say nothing to anyone.
Destroy this letter.

Bertram

♥❀♥

I dream that a team of eight runs over me
at full gallop.
I wake to the beating of rain.
How can any roof withstand it?
I shiver.
Is Celestia warm?
Is she under a decent roof?
But no!
I must retrain my thoughts.
Her welfare is no longer my concern.

How could she choose this?

I gather the blankets around me
and get up to stir the fire.
The hinged frame sits on the mantel
and I remove Celestia's likeness.

She was such a good girl,
never gave a minute's worry
before last summer.
I was so proud of all the books she read,
and now . . .
nothing.

I tear the portrait
in half,
half again,
and let the pieces fall
into the fire.

Johnstown

Celestia

How long have I been here in Johnstown?
Cannot keep day from night,
caring for two helpless men,
catnapping in Anna's rocker.
I retrieve her sewing from its basket—
how many years untouched?

I shake the dust
and examine the fine needlework,
not unlike what we have been taught.
Her books,
her garden,
her travels . . .

Perhaps Anna's life was once not so different
from mine.
What if she left that life to become a teacher,
and to marry Peter's father.
What did *her* parents do about it?
Was she banished like Estrella?

I wonder
what Estrella is stitching at this moment
somewhere abroad.
I wish I had applied myself to lessons—
instead of sneaking a book
under my embroidery frame—
so we could be sewing at the same time.
Joined in spirit at least.

I imagine the woman in the portrait
working her needle like Estrella,
gracefully,
rhythmically.

Sleep prevails again.
I dream Estrella
hums and rocks
a baby.
A loving embrace,
warm and dry,
safe.
Longing for my sister

nearly wakes me . . .
surely she has delivered by now . . .
but sleep overpowers.

When my eyes open next
from a crazy-quilt nest on the cot,
Peter is whistling
and stirring a pot on the stove.

He looks over and smiles.
His vigor is returning.
I smile back.
I can tell
he is glad I am here.

May 31, 1889

South Fork Fishing and Hunting Club
Lake Conemaugh

Whitcomb

8:00 a.m.
Givens lurks outside the dining room
until I finish breakfast. "The team is hitched
and the carriage is waiting for you, sir."
I glance at my pocket watch—"I did not order a carriage"—
and move past him.
"Well, I thought you might have a mind
to drive down and fetch your daughter."
Of all the meddling . . .
I stop short,
one foot on the stair. "Mr. Givens, I have no daughter.
In the future, you will remember that."

11:00 a.m.
Another disturbance!
Shouting . . .
men's voices.
I hate to leave my work,
but I push back from the desk
and follow the sound to the dam,
finding the kind of operation
I would never tolerate under my direction.

The lake has risen to the top of the dam.
Workers shovel rocks and dirt
while the young engineer employed by the club
rides a horse over the crest
and yells orders.

It's been raining forever.
Shouldn't they have started sooner?

A crowd of onlookers has gathered.
A local man leans toward me. "I been telling them
all morning to pull out those screens over the spillway."
"Screens?" I glance toward the spillway
cascading through solid bedrock
on the far side of the dam.
The lake is so high,

yet the waterfall
looks only slightly heavier than usual.

"You folks put in screens
to keep the lake stocked with fish.
Now the screens won't budge—
they're all packed with branches and logs
coming downstream from the storm."
"So what does that mean?" I glance toward the valley.
"The spillway's clogged
and there's no other outlet."
"No other outlet? Are there no valves or pipes?"
The man from South Fork shakes his head. "Used to be."
"That cannot be right.
There must be some mistake."
"Right or not, what I *can* tell you
is all that water has to go somewhere."

⤫✦⤪

12:00 noon
The engineer on horseback announces
he has decided against
opening another spillway through the dam
to slow the emptying of the lake.
That action would ultimately *destroy* the dam—
best to let nature take the blame.
"I took the warning to the South Fork wire myself.

The valley has surely sounded the alarm hours ago.
We have done what we could." He turns his horse,
muttering about his dinner,
and gallops back to the clubhouse.

❧

12:30 p.m.
A smooth sheet of water
pours over the center of the dam
like cream from a tipped pitcher.

Even a businessman from the city
knows water going *over* a dam
means that dam is about to fail!
And a few men with shovels
will not succeed in holding back
three miles of reservoir.

Thousands of people live in that valley,
and my daughter is certainly among them.

❧

2:45 p.m.
The mood of the crowd changes
as water sprouts
from the face of the dam

and washes away riprap,
the rocks tumbling down
toward the valley.
Workers have dismantled the bridge
over the spillway.
There is nothing left to do.
Everyone moves off the dam
to the sides
to wait,
to watch.

Several boulders roll away—
then more leaks.
Once the water gets a taste
for moving,
nothing can stop it.

A notch appears,
a trough
gouged
by lake water.
I can no longer hear voices now;
the rush uses up all the sound in the world.

Soon the better part of the dam just melts,
disappears.
The water cannot get out fast enough,
far enough.

My head cannot hold the roar—
no room in it for thought.

***

3:46 p.m.
Just shy of an hour
the lake is gone,
past a bend in the valley.
Silence is such a surprise.
My ears hum.

Workers climb down into the muck
to gather flapping fish.
Those precious fish
held in by screens
that helped the dam fail—
some sport to fetch them now.

***

3:50 p.m.
The lake is empty
and my mind is empty of rational thought.

All I have are tormented visions
of what that rush of lake water
is doing to my daughter
right now.

I can only wish Celestia
were right here with me,
so I could know she was safe—
I would not even care
what juvenile rebellions
she might be planning.
But this fretful wish
comes with the dark twin of knowing
I alone am responsible
for driving her away.

Fear
commands my arms and legs
to find my daughter—
fear that it is too late,
but also dread and regret,
and a need to know if she is alive or dead.

Though I cannot get ahead of the flood
and save her,
my irrational impulse is to try.

I begin to descend;
the other men try to hold me back, shouting,
"What's the matter with you, Whitcomb?"
"The road's washed away!" another yells.
I can barely form words,
something between a growl and a moan
escapes my throat:

"My daughter's down there."
"Sorry." They release me. "Good luck—
stay up high or you'll drown in mud."

I pick my way through the trees
and tangles of branches
above the
washed-bare
valley floor.

I hear the men's voices above me
echoing off the stone corridor: "Poor bastard.
Who knows what he'll find."
"If he even makes it there alive.
It's fifteen miles to Johnstown and hell in every step."

The mountain walls are ripped down to rock
over fifty feet up.

I am an hour behind the lake—
whatever is done
is long done now.

East Conemaugh

Kate

3:35 p.m.
Last year, a train took me to nursing school,
and that was fitting.
Today, another train carries me to a new job
further east.
All east-bound trains are halted,
have been the better part of the day.
Make lists in my head to pass the time:
supplies the new boss might need,
symptoms of various ailments,
names of bones and such.
Time will prove if it is a good match—

don't believe in fate.
Just hard work.

Rain impedes our progress.
Cars shift around in the train yard.
Waiting is something for which I have a talent;
however, the body does not like to sit so long.

One foot pauses on the last step;
one foot pauses over the mud.
The hushed voices of the conductor and the brakeman
meet my ears:
"Washout near Buttermilk Falls
up the line.
Nothing to do but wait." The conductor's voice is low.
"Railroad'll get someone down to fix it.
Probably take the rest of the day, though."
The brakeman spits.

The conductor's voice carries
in the direction of the train yard,
"All that Cambria iron
and human ingenuity
don't amount to beans
when all this water puts its mind to it."
"Speaking of which"—the brakeman clears his throat,
but his voice still shakes a bit—
"do you pay any mind
to talk of that dam giving way?"

"Same story year after year
and it always holds.
Some folks think it's funny
to get you riled up."
"Just the same,
it wouldn't hurt to be prepared." The brakeman spits again.

"I won't be responsible for what happens
if you strike panic in these people"—
the conductor whistles softly—
"like caged animals."
"Well, I suppose a railcar *is* the safest place
they could be."
"Sure, you know how heavy that thing is."

3:38 p.m.
Always think of myself as the sensible type.
Not one to fix on
the brakeman's worries.
Trust what I can see and hear
with my own eyes and ears.
Trust the solid ground beneath my feet.
Wouldn't have put any stock in the idea of
rats leaving a sinking ship,
but I swear I have a moment
of some kind of animal sense
that says to get off that train.

Now!
But maybe it has more to do with this:
since the sight of Early
drowned dead beneath the footbridge
was forever lodged in my nightmares,
I am deathly afraid of water.

3:39 p.m.
Thinking of so much lake water
up in the mountains above us
gets these legs moving.
My feet barely touch the wet earth.
The railroad men yell, "Miss! You'll be soaked!"
and start after me,
but I clear the ditch
and break for the incline.

Run out of hillside,
can go no further,
climb a tree,
gasping for breath,
wondering what it felt like
for Early,
if he was even aware.

The branches crack
and bow

beneath my weight.
Heart slows its pounding.
Must look plenty silly,
a respectable woman,
a trained nurse,
squatting in a tree.
Almost laugh.
Almost.

Straighten my collar
and smooth my shirtwaist.
Plan my excuses to the other passengers.

Feet
slippery with silty mud
search out a lower branch.

Just then, a train whistle,
tied down,
wails
from up the line
in the direction of that old dam.

Thunder falls toward us
from high up the mountain pass.
Breath and screams
leave the lungs
all at once.
Fingernails dig into the tree

and my face buries itself
in the wet trunk.

It's coming.
The water is on its way
and I am already drowning.

Maura

3:39 p.m.
At first I think the long whistle is just for me,
a love song.
I smile to myself,
hands to hot cheeks.

But it doesn't end,
getting closer
too quickly,
and still it doesn't end.

My skin prickles
all over
remembering Joseph's stories
of the screaming fairies
who shriek in the dooryard
right before someone inside dies.

Their sound couldn't be
more horrible than this.

So loud now
I wonder if he is bringing the train
right for us
off the tracks
cutting through fields of mud.

I gather the children
into my skirts
to hide them from the blare,
to hide them from the banshee.

⸙

3:40 p.m.
The children's whimpers
are lost in the shrill whistle,
but I can see their lips curl,
their eyes pleading.

My life has been about saving things:
the pinch of sugar
that becomes the birthday cake;
the scraps of cloth
that become the quilt to warm our sleep
or the rug to cushion our feet;

the bird baby that falls from its cozy nest in the eaves,
soft as fog where its feathers should be.
I feed it with a wet rag.
Even the stitching I make with my needles,
each knot more secure than the last,
holding my love tightly
in its woolen grip,
each stitch
a moment of my time,
a breath of my life,
to create a fabric
my loved ones
will remember me by . . .

But the stitches are slipping
and I feel row after row
ripping
unpopping
faster
faster
unfastening
at last
unraveling.

I imagine
the dam crumbling,
the lake bursting,
and floodwater rising around us,
destroying all the good we've made.

But this awful noise has come to warn us,
perhaps to say this flood will *not* be the gradual
seeping tide we all expected,
but perhaps something more like a crashing wave.
It suddenly dawns so clear,
the terrible power of moving water
and the need to run for the hillside
in peril for our lives.

And this is the moment
that will live inside me
all my life,
maybe for eternity:
I can't save it—
my house,
my geraniums,
my handiwork—
and I can't stay
for the love of it.
My children must live
and I must live
for them.

Kate

3:40 p.m.
Eyes closed,
waiting for it to be over,
don't want to think of the other train passengers:
man with a cane,
foolish women with frilly hats,
bored children,
not to mention the townspeople . . .
so many people . . .
and they're going to need help
getting to higher ground.

Force air into the lungs.
Knees shimmy down the tree.
Fears be damned!

❧

3:42 p.m.
Didn't think much could surprise me in life
anymore,
but when I'm old and gray
on my deathbed
and I close my eyes the last time,
I will still see this sight:
an entire town
at my feet
disappears.

Maura

3:42 p.m.
Leaving takes me over.

I lift the tiny baby from the cradle
and tie him to my chest with a shawl.
He sleeps undisturbed.

I tie up my skirts,
preparing to run,
and replace a loose hairpin with shaking fingers,
still knotting
until the last.

One final look
at all I swept
and cleaned
and created—
the daily doings,
sweat and toil
of a humble country girl,
one like any other—
it pales
and blurs
before my eyes.
It is nothing now.

One baby strapped to my belly,
another on each hip,

and the oldest clinging to my skirt,
I leave it all behind,
not bothering to shut the door,
a silent offering
to the invader that is surely on its way:
Take it all,
just not these babies.
We cross the street
against the rain
and begin the climb uphill.
My arms and legs burn from the effort.
The children are much put out.

Neighbors climb with us
and a woman with long braids
who I do not recognize
helps me with the little ones.
Strangers jump from railcars,
some with bags
and umbrellas.
They jump the ditch to follow us.

All these townspeople,
all these railway passengers
saved
by Joseph's warning,
and I would trade them all
for him.

Kate

3:43 p.m.
Looking down from the hill
at the East Conemaugh train yard:
a roundhouse,
towers,
sheds,
extra locomotives
and cars . . .
and, pointed east,
two sections
of the *Day Express*
parked alongside each other,
and the mail train,
waiting out the rain.

When folks hear the blare
of that engine whistle tied down,
I see it they got two choices:
run for the hills
or stay put and pray
that a train car is the safest place to be.

Passengers
of the first section of the *Day Express*
choose to run.
Problem is,
the length of the second section

now stands between them
and the hill.
Most folks crawl under,
some climb over,
a few run the length and around.
Next problem:
a ten-foot ditch wild with runoff.
Folks make the leap,
or jump in and climb out the other side,
or throw each other in.
Some never make it out.

Eyeing the mud,
a few return to their seats.
Two fancy-dressed girls go back,
my guess is, for their overshoes.
Won't need them where they're going.

Passengers
from the second section of the *Day Express*
choose to stay put,
except the folks in one sleeper car
who choose to run.

Passengers
of the mail train
choose to run.
Everyone exits
in an orderly fashion

with the assistance of the trainmen,
like a well-rehearsed dance.
They negotiate the ditch,
climb the hill
to safety.

People from the houses
run uphill, too.
A girl my age
is much burdened with babies,
so I grab the two middle-sized,
one under each arm,
trying to lead her on shaking legs
up the muddy hillside.

The girl stops short
as the engine with the tied-down whistle
comes round the bend
into town,
screams that she knows the sound
of her husband's whistle.

Maura

3:44 p.m.
I hand the baby to a neighbor,
pry loose the older one's fingers,

and run for the engine.
Friends try to hold me back,
tearing my dress and my flesh,
but I am fierce
and they don't expect it.

I peer up the tracks
and thank God
I see the light of Joseph's locomotive
coming toward the train yard,
but the next sight
drops me to my knees
right there on the rails.

Behind the train
trees sway violently
in a tumbling thunder
like a storm coming up from the ground
or a tornado on its side.
The lake water can't be far behind,
coming on fast.
Will the engine be faster?

3:45 p.m.
Around the last bend
in the mountain pass
before East Conemaugh
the mystery comes clear.

A dark mass fills the valley,
coming down fast,
racing the train.

The big powerful locomotive
suddenly looks small
and my big powerful husband
is helpless.

The whistle fills my ears
but the roar and the rumble
fill my whole body
and the ground beneath
with quaking.

The mail train and two passenger trains
block the way.
His engine slows.
I cover my ears
and run toward it,
slipping in the mud,
my knees bloody,
my hair loose in my eyes.

When he sees me
stumbling toward him,
Joseph skips the stairs
and jumps from the cab.
We roll together,

head for the rise,
crawl and scratch up the rocks.
Fear pins us to a tree,
arms around each other and the trunk.
With only a heartbeat to spare,
the thing is upon us.

It is some time before we see water.
First is churning
trees
poles
fences
barns
and houses.
Then the valley is a river—
a boiling soup
of buildings
horses
cows
and people,
some clinging to rooftops
or logs,
some floating
already still.

The torrent lifts my husband's locomotive
and whirls it
off down the valley.

Our little white frame house
with the front porch,
nesting birds,
and baskets of red geraniums,
lifts off its moorings,
rides with the current awhile
before spinning
and splintering.

I saved what I could,
what matters:
I look further uphill
to my babies,
who watch with interest
but without understanding.
Kind neighbors
and the helpful stranger
hold them safe,
but their wide eyes
and outstretched arms
say they want only me.
And Joseph.
The town below
is beyond their concern.

We work our way toward them.
I reach for them
with a need to kiss every inch

and cling
and weep
and rejoice
that we all made it out alive.
And that we're together.

 .

Kate

3:45 p.m.

It's a thirty-foot wave when it hits,
taking apart section one of the *Day Express*.
The cars swirl off with the water;
some catch fire.

The big roundhouse where trains are stored
deflects the flood
for section two of the *Day Express*.
The flood moves the train cars forward
and back on the track,
fills and empties them of water,
but no one from section two is harmed
except for those
who tried to run.
One man has a cane and a limp.

Another fellow carries him
for a stretch,
but drops him
to make the hill
with only a second to spare.

The mail train itself
is trapped under a fallen telegraph tower,
which keeps it from being swept on down the valley.

The baggage master doesn't make it to the hill,
but climbs on one of the train yard's engines.
When the water moves on,
the one he chose is the only train yard engine left standing,
the others toppled,
or strewn about.
Everyone from the mail train survives.

Maura

3:53 p.m.
Joseph and I form a circle
around the children
on the muddy slope.
I check every limb for soundness
over and over again,

count every finger and toe
the way I did when they were born.
The baby sleeps.
The girls hide their faces in their father's shoulders.
The oldest can't stop crying and hiccupping.
His face is hot and streaked,
but his eyes are fresh out of tears.
His open mouth against my neck,
he grabs a hank of my hair
too hard,
like he'll never let go.
And I don't want him to,
no matter how much it hurts.
Terror has broken my heart
in two:
equal parts
bitter and sweet.

3:55 p.m.
When the beast has roared past,
the relative quiet
is too loud.

Watching the tail of it
whip toward Johnstown,
we know it isn't over yet

for our neighbors below,
where the population is greater.

Those of us
so grateful to be safe on the hillside
are silent with prayer
for the people of Johnstown
in their last moments of not knowing.

Kate

3:55 p.m.
Looking back
at what is left of East Conemaugh,
knowing the need
will be greatest in Johnstown proper,
I hurry down the line,
up on the ridge,
quick as the mud and fallen trees allow.

Johnstown

Celestia

4:00 p.m.
Johnstown appears shut down
with rain.
I abandon my craving for fresh bread
and turn back,
empty-handed,
soaked to the waist.

"Peter, the rivers are rising.
The streets are canals.
People are poling skiffs!"
I wring out my skirts and coat as I stand on the doorstep.
Peter grins. "Welcome to Johnstown."

"Some families are moving to higher ground."
"This is how it is
to live in a valley
where three rivers cross paths."

"But your neighbors say it has never been this high before."
"Water comes up to the front step
but it never comes in the door." He takes my coat
and spreads it over the rocker by the fire.

I rub my hands near the stove
but cannot shake the chill. "I have a bad feeling."
"Are you thinking about
the dam?" Peter shakes out a blanket
around my shoulders and bundles it under my chin.

"What if the dam really *is* flawed?"
"Didn't you say yourself they'd fix it
if it needed fixing?" Peter smiles and studies my face.

"What if they just don't know very much about dams?"
"They'd hire somebody that knows about dams. Right?"
"Well, supposedly they *did*." I shrug the blanket tighter.
"Club members are powerful men," he says.
"They wouldn't be who they are
if they didn't handle their affairs responsibly."
Peter wraps my hands
around a hot mug of broth.
Twists of steam sting my cheeks

and cloud my eyes.
I want so much to let him convince me,
to stay here in this moment:
warm fire,
warm blanket,
warm embrace . . .
but . . .

"I've *seen* how they *handle their affairs*!
How they deal with their own flesh and blood,
how my parents dealt with Estrella!"
My eyes fill with tears.
How I miss Estrella!
I put down the mug and blink.
Peter nods, suddenly serious. "What do you want to do?"

"Plan and prepare."
Peter reaches for firewood. "We could leave in the morning."
I place my hand on his arm. "We should leave tonight."
"What about Papa?"

"We'll carry him together
on a board or plank or . . ." I glance around the tiny room.
"How about that door?" Peter points to the bedroom door.

I grab the fire poker
to knock off the hinges. "Do you think
we can make it to the hills?"

"I know a man with a wagon . . .
maybe we can stay with one of Papa's mining friends
up on Prospect Hill."
"Good"—
the flimsy hinges give way—
"and we can bring our food to share,
maybe a gift, too. Do you have any whisky?"
Peter and I wrestle the door from its frame.
It breaks free all at once.
Peter, the door, and I land in a heap.
"Celestia!" Peter pretends to be shocked
as I squirm out from under the door. "Whisky?"
I roll my eyes and make a face. "For your father's friends."

❧

4:07 p.m.
Down the lane
someone is shouting.
I peer through raindrops on the windowpane.
People are running.
A distant rumbling shakes in my ears,
punctuated by crashing.

Could it be . . . ?

"Peter! The dam must have gone out!"

His eyes go wide. "Run!"

"No. We'll carry your father together." I look for a spot
to lay the door flat
so we can rest him on it.

Peter disappears into the bedroom.
The roar is louder.
The cracking is closer.
Screams begin
and end suddenly.

Peter stands in the doorway,
his father over his shoulder.
Our eyes meet.

Beams creak.
The house shifts and moans.
A splitting sound
begins a bubbling in the floor.
I startle
and jump on the rocker.
Another hole
lets a geyser spray.

We start for the front door,
but with a great heaving sound,
the floor comes up to meet us.

4:09 p.m.
It is upon us all at once.
The floorboards are rolling waves.
The house rocks and swirls.
Oily brackish liquid surges and billows.
With a crack,
Peter and his father
rise on a gusher
far above me.
The last instant is all Peter's eyes
trying to hold on to me
with the strength of sight.
Then the men disappear—
that fast—
and the house is suddenly no more,
only me
and this door
to prove it ever existed.

4:10 p.m.
Water closes in on all sides,
darkness,
a roof peak perhaps
above me.

The sum of life
tallies itself
in that moment before certain death.
Mine reads:
a good life
honest
loved
no regrets,
even if finding Peter
has been the death of me.

I breathe my last fill of putrid air
as I see a patch of light.
It cannot be the glow of heaven yet,
while my chest still bursts with breath.

Peter

4:10 p.m.
Papa and I are lifted skyward
as the house folds up
beneath us—
Celestia!

All around is movement:
objects
people

pieces of houses
stopping
starting
swirling
in the mix.
Nothing like water,
it is an avalanche of wreckage.

I tighten my grip on Papa's wrist
as we join the current.
I kick to keep us afloat
but crosscurrents compete
and we spin.

I hear a dull thud,
loud,
close.
Before the impact
travels down my body
to my toes,
even before the pain registers,
everything goes black.

Celestia

4:11 p.m.
Knuckles white,
gripping the wood—

Peter's door
will surely be my raft
to the other side.

Sounds muffle,
air bubbles,
light ripples
above me
and opens.
Somehow
I break surface
for another gasp
of brown mist.

The door and I bob up
and float—
a different boat
on Lake Conemaugh—
before the rapids
spirit us away.

Houses sail by,
people on the rooftops.
Some spin,
some get stuck,
some fold up
and sink:
house
roof

people
and all.

A locomotive rears up
and slams down:
a new ripple
to redirect my little craft.

People wave from attic windows
and try to reach me
with broom handles
or throw me ropes,
but I am moving so fast
and bumping over things
that I do not dare take a hand off the door.
I long for their comfort
in numbers
but I have seen what can happen to a house
in an instant.
Are they truly safe?
Are they any safer than I am?

Mostly I want the sides,
the hills.
I can see people there,
some of them dry,
some of them climbing out of the mess.
If I found a stick or a board,
would I dare attempt to paddle?

I picture another boat,
another time,
paddling on the lake—
Estrella singing—
this calms me a bit.
I struggle for the words,
the tune,
anything—
the lanterns,
the fireflies,
her face.
I want to see her.
I *will* see her.
I resolve to walk out of this.
Climb,
crawl,
or hobble out of this.
Peter is likely dead.
But I will live
to find Estrella
and her baby.

4:35 p.m.
The water is slower now.
My little raft and I have bounced
all around town
and I have seen fickle fate

splinter crafts more seaworthy than mine.
And I have seen rescues of travelers
more hopeless.

A large woman with braids
like bundles of flax
directs a pack of men to knot rope bridges
and lay planks across the wreckage.
They pass children up to her on the hill.
I wish I could be one of them,
turned over to the capable hands of
someone who could so quickly
make order out of chaos,
but my raft is drifting in a tide pool of sorts,
away from that trajectory.

The door and I are moored
against a bank of debris,
out of the torrent
but not secure enough to walk across.
I must leave the relative safety
of this temporary harbor
and rejoin the rushing falls
to have any hope
of navigating over to the rescuers.

I tighten my grip
with shaking raw fingers
and push off the rubble

with my feet—
stripped of shoes
overshoes
and stockings.
How little I dare extend
either leg for fear of tipping the raft!
Sometimes only a toe touches
barrel
wagon
weathervane.
How slowly I creep.
How wet and cold
and alone.
The grunting
I hear
is my own sobs
choking in my throat.
I am
too frightened for tears.

4:37 p.m.
I ride the door
back into the fray,
heading for the men
leaning down from the plank bridges.
One calls and holds out a hand.
I must stand to reach it,

must balance in the water
and risk my door,
which has saved me
thus far,
maybe even jump
at the last second
for a chance
at five human fingers.

I force myself to wait
until the moment is right,
pull my knees up under me
crouch
wobble
wobble
then jump.

"Got her!" the man yells.
His hand is warm
and padded with calluses.
But my jump
has caused the door
to shoot out from under me
too suddenly.
My weight is thrown forward,
ripping my hand from his grip.

The splash cuts across my face.
I will not sink

but move with the current.
My destination is clear:
the crush of houses
barns
steeples
and stores
colliding ahead.

The woman with the pale braids
is at the water's edge,
leaning forward like the prow of a ship,
her waist tied with rope.
She jumps just ahead of me
and I tumble into her grasp.
We lurch toward shore
one tug at a time
as the others reel us in.

But my savior is suddenly my captor:
she clings to me,
strangling,
dragging me under.

What an odd kind of bravery,
one that could kill us both.

I pry
push
fight for breath.

Her arms are locked
around my neck and head.
The men shout,
dragging us,
separating us.
She is frozen shut with shock.
They carry her off.

I press my face
to the dirt and rock.
I want to put my arms around the hill
and swallow it.
I want to be the land—
on it,
in it,
never leave it.

I curl up and hug myself.
A stranger wraps his coat around me
and carries me uphill.
I feel gratitude.
I feel relief.
But I will never again feel safe.

4:50 p.m.
Solid earth is not long beneath me
before I learn

those of us sound in body
are putting aside whatever soundness of mind
has been compromised
to rescue those still struggling
in the morass.

Or assist those already hillside,
cold,
wet,
wandering in confusion.

Or comfort those who have already glimpsed
the first depth
of their unfathomable loss.

South Fork

Whitcomb

Evening
Leaving behind what was Lake Conemaugh,
I follow South Fork Creek
toward town.

I steel myself as South Fork comes into view.
Mostly built into the hillside,
South Fork has suffered less damage
than I expected.
Citizens are in shock nonetheless,
and I overhear:
"The planing mill."
"The bridge,

the grocery,
and the barbershop."
"My house!"
"My business!"
Someone counts twenty buildings and houses lost.
"One caboose and four train cars."
Lives lost can be counted on one hand.

They recall
the man on horseback from the club
bringing the warning,
but no one put much store by it.
Like other warnings
other years.

No one at the depot
remembers seeing a well-dressed girl
board the train
a few days back,
but then,
everybody is looking for somebody
right now.

I cannot tarry long
if I want to make Mineral Point
before dark.

Conemaugh Valley

.

Whitcomb

Evening
I follow South Fork Creek
to where it joins the Little Conemaugh.
I recall the river valley as a deep channel
all the way
to Johnstown,
the railroad staying close by the water.
I peer through the trees
for any sign of the tracks
that once carried my family and me
home to Pittsburgh,
that in all probability carried Celestia
away from me
and into . . .
God only knows what destiny.

Mineral Point

Whitcomb

Night
The only hint that a town
of thirty white frame houses
once stood
on this plane
of bare rock
is the cluster of people
scrambling to make order of the debris,
to cobble together makeshift housing
before night falls hard.

If the citizens of Mineral Point wonder at
a stranger stumbling into their midst

looking as stunned and wild-eyed as themselves,
who happens to possess a box of dry matches,
they do not question it.
Perhaps they chalk it up
to a well-deserved miracle.

I offer up my coat
to a shivering woman
who has lost her daughter.

I roll up my shirtsleeves—
I am no stranger to labor,
I tell myself,
mine was a hardscrabble youth—
and search out the driest kindling
to pass the night here.

The woman's husband has gone off
to search for the body.
All I can do for her
is stoke the fire
and sit beside her
and her pain.

The people of Mineral Point, who had very little
and lost it all,
share what they can gather
and make a place for me by the fire.
People are decent.
Rich or poor, they won't let me die out here.

Johnstown

Peter

Night
Rolling
and rolling,
searching,
cresting
with each wave,
but never advancing . . .
My eyes open
to stillness
in a strange building.
Memories line up.
A moan escapes.

"Don't move"—a voice cuts the dark—
"The house could go any second."
"Where am I?" I make out a profile
against a faint glow through a window.
"You are in my attic. Butler's the name.
You ran aground my porch roof and I hauled you in."
"And my father? I was carrying him."
"Sorry, my boy. You were unconscious.
Looks like a nasty bump on your forehead."
I touch the tender spot and wince.
No time for pain—I must find Papa.
I must find Celestia.
Where to start?
"And what is the address here, Mr. Butler?"
"I would have had a different answer this morning, son,
but tonight my address is
the middle of South Fork Reservoir."

With pain and effort,
I raise my head
to see above the sill,
and there it is,
an entire lake
standing in Johnstown,
only a few building tops,
steeples and a clock tower,
poking out of the surface.
An entire lake

beneath this attic window,
and the orange flicker
reflecting in every drop
and lighting the terrible night
is a fire
at the stone bridge.

Celestia

Night
Darkness falls too soon
and a new, nameless dread
insinuates itself:
a flickering,
a fog of wood smoke,
and the scent of singeing
flesh and hair.

The big stone bridge
is a new dam
for Lake Conemaugh,
a logjam of debris—
even whole houses
with stoves still lighted,
soaking in floodwater infused with fuel—
and now the whole mess
is aflame.

I am unsure how long
the fire
has been burning
across one end of town,
but the voice in my head
grows more urgent,
saying I must hurry and find Peter.
If he is alive,
he might need help
and I may very well be the only person
looking for him.

Night
I look into every
soot- and smoke-blackened face
as I near the bridge.

Some eyes search my face in return.
Others see nothing.

How can such a fire
rise out of so much water?
Like the water itself is on fire.

Houses are piled on top of each other.
People climb out of windows
and scramble across the smoldering mountain

of buildings,
train cars,
trees,
all sewn up tight in miles of wire.
They head for the bridge.

Others simply jump
when the flames are too close.
Their fate is less kind
and they cannot be reached
by rescuers.

I peer through the smoke,
though it stings my eyes.
I can do nothing to help these people
and none of them is Peter.

Fire stretches into the blackness.
Coughing,
bare feet blistering,
I stumble in retreat.

AFTER THE FLOOD

East Conemaugh

Maura

The night is so long and cold
with these babies
and no food
for the morning.
Nothing dry to burn.

The loss settles over us:
no roof over our heads
to keep off the rain,
no pillow to lay our weariness upon,
no cross-stitch welcoming us home,
no canning or pickling.
No story quilt to wrap around us
and tell us who we are.

I gnash my teeth—
oh, why didn't I think to grab
the baby's favorite toy?
I can live without my comforts
but what else does *he* have?
Picturing it in my mind:
stuffed rag bear,
smiling,
wide-eyed,
taunting me . . .
forsaken
in the cradle . . .
only a memory now.

Johnstown

Peter

Dreaming in voices
as the sky changes to a lighter gray,
I realize we are a group
in Mr. Butler's attic:
several women, another man, and Butler.
I open my eyes with effort
to see many eyes staring back at me,
inspecting me,
preparing to move me.

Save yourselves.
Leave me here.
Everyone I love is surely dead.

My vision fades.
Butler lifts my feet
and two hands go under my arms.
I pass out again.

I dream Butler and the others pick their way across the rubble,
the water having subsided.
The two men carry me.
Or is it a dead man?

The men would move faster without me,
their balance better,
but they press on.

I feel gratitude—
such a kind gesture,
but unnecessary—
I strain to tell them it is too late.

Kate

No equipment.
Next to nothing for supplies.
But they're calling me and a few damp blankets a medical station.
So they bring in this fella
about dawn,
more dead than alive—

a serious blow to the head
and a night cold and wet in an attic
surrounded by all that filthy water.
It doesn't look good.

The boy comes round
then blacks out again,
yet he didn't drown
in forty feet of water!
Early drowned in ten inches—
a stream that wouldn't come over your boot.
Doesn't make sense.
Different circumstances,
but their fate's the same.
Some other girl will be the widow now
and her life will become a burden
like mine. . . .
No.
Find the driest blanket.
Do what I can.
He must live.

Johnstown

Celestia

The night has malingered,
dripping cold
in spite of the fire's heat.

Daybreak is a formality.
There is no sun to speak of,
only eventual illumination.

Heavy cloud cover
settles on the backs of nearby mountains,
making the valley a corridor.
Sounds echo off the sky
and my voice rings in my ears

as I inquire of every survivor:
"Have you seen a man
about this high?
Brown hair?
Do you know Peter?"

Mineral Point

Whitcomb

Waking, stiff-limbed,
I am the first to see the silhouette
in the murky morning light—
a man
carrying a girl child
limp against his shoulder.
A hoarse cry comes from deep within the woman's body
as she stumbles to her feet.
I brace myself for the sadness,
dreading what might await me further down the line.
But
the girl lifts her head
and the woman shrieks in surprise.

The three fall in a heap of crying and rocking.
I turn away,
my eyes prickling with tears,
some for the little family
and even more for my own.

East Conemaugh

Whitcomb

I bid the girl and her parents goodbye
and resume slow progress
down the river valley.
Muddy,
tired,
hungry,
and anxious,
I arrive in the borough of East Conemaugh,
a larger town,
home of the train yard.
Everyone speaks with gratitude
of an engine driver
who sounded the alarm

with his whistle tied down.
His house is one of a hundred or so lost.
His locomotive is among hundreds
of train cars scattered about
or carried off by the flood
as it picked up speed
toward Johnstown.
And toward Celestia.

Johnstown

Celestia

The valley is a mud puddle:
sky gray,
earth brown,
debris to match.
Standing water
reflecting it all.

The stench confuses
the gnawing in my stomach.
It will be quite a long time,
I assume,
before any of us

tastes food or clean water.
Such hunger,
such need,
and
so much work to be done.

Small pockets of organization form:
morgues
in the schoolhouse
and the saloon.

The fear of finding Peter
among the dead
tugs against
the dread of never knowing.
I concentrate only on placing
one bare foot ahead of the other.

Stranger after stranger
lined up in rows,
laid across desks.
I hurry through the aisle
covering my nose and mouth
with my borrowed sleeve.

I try to outrun the stagnant air
and reach the schoolhouse door,
but the whole of Johnstown
is no better.

I pause just long enough
for a thought to take root,
and I turn back.

My search had been
for the remains of a young man,
for Peter,
whom I did not find . . .
but still, some faint recognition
nudges at my mind.
I go back
to the familiar features
on the face of an older man.

He has no look of struggle
about him.
The cough had taken the fight out of him
long before the water came.

Peter's father.

Kate

People from the hills,
they bring what they have:
dry things,
food,

tinctures,
or spirits.
The latter sterilizes
scrounged
or improvised
tools—
at least in this camp.

Another stick
on the paltry fire,
smoldering pieces of chairs,
kindling,
whatever could be carried
or spared
from the few households
on higher ground.

Patients stagger in.
Some are carried.
I tend burns,
torn flesh,
broken bones.

Broken spirits—
know nothing of fixing those.
Send them on to the preacher.

Wake the boy
from time to time.

Keep him dry
in a lean-to.

He isn't Early,
remind myself.
He'll live
and it won't bring Early back,
but he *will* live.

No hunger.
No sleep.

Only doing.

Woodvale

Whitcomb

I pass through Woodvale,
recalling it as the pride of the valley.
A town built by Cambria Iron:
pretty white houses,
maple-lined avenue,
and horse-drawn streetcars.

Stunned,
numb,
grieving,
citizens of Woodvale have no words.

Woodvale had no warning.

Most of a woolen mill,
a tannery,
two schoolhouses,
the streetcar shed with dozens of horses
and tons of hay,
the wire works, and
hundreds of houses
are gone.

One out of every three people in Woodvale is dead.

I cannot bear to wonder
if I will find anyone alive in Johnstown.
I hurry on.

Johnstown

Kate

Don't need answers—
Who did this thing?
Why'd this happen to me?—
and such.
Some folks will make themselves crazy
wrapping their heads around it.

Just see broken bodies
and fix them,
if I can.

Just see need
and answer it

with
will,
muscle,
endurance,
bearing up.
Those are the only answers I need.

No mountainful of water
can beat me down.

Celestia

Wandered all day.
The second night threatens
to be worse.
Talk of thieves
and disease.

Cannot take another step.

Darkness inside
rivals the gloom,
fog,
dusk.

I am attracted by sounds of bustling
and the warm glow

of a lantern.
I find myself again
in the domain
of calm,
efficient
strength—
the woman with the heavy rope braids.
The woman who saved me
by almost drowning me.

I want to restore her pride
after seeing her moment of weakness.
I sense that weakness would be intolerable to her.

"Hello!" I interrupt her chopping up a chair.
She drops the little ax and turns,
straightens her shoulders,
smoothes her apron,
waits.

"I . . . uh . . . you saved me yesterday. . . ."
Nothing.
I try again: "I want to thank you. . . ."
No response.
"Celestia Whitcomb." I hold out my hand.

Her eyes narrow.
Her hands remain at her sides. "Kate."

"Don't recall you, Miss.
Went into shock myself
for a spell."

I withdraw my hand. "Well, you *did* save me, Kate.
And I want to repay you."

"Don't want your money."

I hold up the shreds of my petticoats and shrug. "I have no—"
how absurd everything suddenly seems—
"I have no *pockets*."
I bite my lip to hold back a smile.

Kate raises an eyebrow. "Nor shoes neither."
We look at each other,
exhausted,
unreal,
on the verge
of sharing a laugh,
a desperately needed release.

The first tremor ripples through me,
a snort escapes,
but I sense how quickly laughter will give way to tears,
how the shaking will shatter me
into a million scattered pieces.

Kate stiffens again.
"Well, if you've got strength for foolishness,
you've got strength for work.
Lend a hand."

I follow her to the fire.
She hands me a bundle from the hills,
an armload of petticoats—
fresh,
white,
starched—
a great deal better than what I'm wearing.
"Rip these," she says, "and boil them for bandages."
I regard my own garment—
torn,
frayed,
and wet.
The irony tickles again
and my eyes sting
with overwrought tears
unshed.

Kate sets a chipped pot
on a grate fashioned with barrel hoops and wire.
"Don't drink anything not boiled
and don't touch the dead."

Peter

The hands.
The voice.
My lifeline.

I bring myself round
every so often,
when she comes by
to hold my eyelids open
with her quick tough fingers
and peer into my eyes.
I struggle to recognize this face:
the sandy freckles,
like a spotted mare.
Then she frees me with a grunt: "Good."

I am a good boy.

I know only that I want to go home.
What's become of my home?
Is someone waiting for me there?

I may never know,
but I keep reaching
for the
voice
and
the
hands.

Celestia

The quiet desolation
of the valley
is *too* quiet.
Has no one heard of the devastation?
Does no one care?

Isolation.
Trains cannot get through.

The lines are all down
indefinitely.

What about my father?
He must know about the flood.
He must have surmised that I am in Johnstown.
Is he wondering if I am dead?
Or am I dead to him already?

Kate finds a man with a horse
who is heading up to South Fork.
I scrounge for dry paper
to send a note.

How to encompass all that has passed
since I tiptoed down those clubhouse stairs?

The man stares
while the nag sighs and chews
and shifts her weight.

⁓❋⁓

Dear Father,

I am alive—if you care to know it.
Tell Mother not to worry.
I love you both.
I hope you still think of me
as
your loving daughter,

Celestia

⁓❋⁓

We feed the patients
as best we can,
Kate carrying a huge pot of watery gruel—
a feast compared to what may be had
in the rest of the valley—
and me ladling into bowls
or spooning into mouths,
boiling the vessels and utensils
between turns.

Our last stop is a tent of sorts—
a tarp draped over a piece of fence,
a patient moaning underneath.
Kate usually goes in alone.
Must be a horrible sight.

This time
Kate lowers the pot,
stretches her back,
and nods toward the tent. "You feed the boy.
Mrs. Davis over there needs a poultice."

My legs ache.
My feet are swollen.
I long to finish
so we can rest
and maybe eat, too.

I bring the lantern
and the tent
comes alive,
flickering inside.

A cry struggles out of me
even before
I completely recognize
my love.
Alive!

Peter!

I would not have believed
before this moment
that any of the tears in Johnstown
would be tears of joy.

Peter

The chasm between
my nightmares
and wakefulness
has not been worth crossing.
What would I wake to?
Remembering all I've lost?

But now, for the first time,
I think Celestia is calling me
to come across.
Is Celestia waiting there for me?
Alive?
Or calling me to the other world?

Or maybe
it's all been just a terrible dream
and I'll open my eyes to find
Celestia rocking in my mother's chair,

watching me sleep.
Same as before.

Celestia

Weary.
Weak.
Waves pass through me.
I wrap my arms around my middle
to hold back the pain.
At least Peter improves.

The man with the mare
returns
with my note
unopened.

"He isn't up there," the man says. "No one is."

Father must have
retreated
to the city,
fearing
a mob,
a vengeance,
thinking nothing
of me.

I am truly disowned.
This is how it feels.

A shiver works through me
and all my heat leaves
through stinging cheeks
and burning eyes.

"Typhoid," Kate says. "It's here."

After all I have survived,
now I should die
to spite them?

My legs fold up beneath me.

Kate

Typhoid.

The standing water
might kill more
than the wave.

Folks doubled over
stumble into camp.
Some too feverish

are carried.
Cordon off a separate section,
extra clean.

The girl has it.

The boy is well enough.
He helps me now,
helps me care for her.

And so they switched places.
The vigil is his.

They get me to thinking,
and I don't like to give in to thinking:
If I was there to see Early die,
maybe
he's been watching over me—
soul dead
in a moving body—
and he doesn't like what he sees.
Maybe
he's pointing me
to lessons.
Maybe Early is saving me
even though I couldn't save him.
Early is pointing me
back to life.

East Conemaugh

Maura

The railroad is good to us,
repairing the tracks
straightaway
so food and water
and the blankets of city folks
can get to us.

Joseph's out on the line now,
since almost the first minute,
finding ways to get the trains through
even if he has to lead the cars
one by one
like skittish horses across a stream.

His work is interrupted every few minutes
by another newspaperman
from a city I will never see
wanting to hear the whole story again,
wanting to know if he's aware that he's a hero
and that important people all over the country
convey invitations to tea.
My Joseph has charming ways, though,
saying, "There's too much work to be done."
That and his smile seem to satisfy the newspapermen.
Just what a hero would say—
I read it in their faces as they scribble.

They shake hands,
tip their silly hats,
and canter down the hill
back to Johnstown.

༺༄༻

Barrels of whisky appear first,
before food or water.
Some of the men indulge in the evenings
at the edge of the camp.
Every man wants to toast my husband,
slap his back
with teary-eyed gratitude
and offers of gifts when we all get back on our feet.
Some nights he doesn't make it home at all—

home being the ring of stones
where I tend my fire
and the pile of dirty blankets I rock our babies to sleep in.
This is my hearth.
Come back to my hearth.

I don't know how much more gratitude I can bear.

Johnstown

Kate

The girl fails,
weaker by the hour.
No cure for typhoid—
just let it run its course.
Even if there was a medicine,
we wouldn't have it *here*.
The plan:
      Keep her clean.
      Offer food
      and water.
      Bring down the fever
      if you can.

No supplies
for even these simple tasks.

The boy makes arrangements
with a family in the hills
who will take them in
so she can die in a bed at least.

Want to say, *Do they know it's contagious?*
But something stops me—
never hesitated to speak good sense before—
I just nod
and he goes off
to find a length of wood for a stretcher.

Maybe something exists beyond good sense,
something about
love,
loss,
dignity
even in death.

Then the trains arrive.

Train cars bring food and water,
donated clothing,
volunteers,
even medicine.

Supplies arrive
before the fever takes her,

before the boy takes her to the hills.
Now, with clean water,
she has at least
a fighting chance
to outlast the illness.

Fate?
Luck?
Not long ago
I would have said that *I* saved her
with knowledge and the strength of my will,
that I saved the boy,
but now I believe they saved each other.
With hope.

If they're alive,
they have hope,
a chance at happiness.

Early has guided my steps
to be here now,
to show me this.

Peter

There are pieces out there
of the house I was born in,

the school where I learned to read,
Mama's books,
my childhood.
Shards.
All still out there
but unrecognizable.

Can't believe I lived through all this
to get back to Celestia
and now I might lose her to fever.
Just before she became insensible,
she whispered, "Your father . . ."
But I knew.
Kate's silence confirms it
and she points to the schoolhouse.

When I get there the men tell me I'm too late.
They had to start the burying right away
to prevent disease.
Like typhoid.
I don't tell them
it didn't help.

❧

I couldn't save him.
Guilt
gives way to rage—

who is responsible
for all this
devastation?

I want to blame the Club.
I'm surprised by how easily
hatred comes to me.
I want to hate them:
pantywaist cowards
hiding behind their big fat pocketbooks.
Why don't they come out and face us?
Tell us why their dam failed.
Tell us why our town disappeared.
Tell me why Papa died.

I want to hate Club members,
but Celestia is one of them
and I can't get far in hating her.
It twists me all in knots.

The object of my anger
appears:
Mr. Whitcomb is
relatively clean,
dry,
but rumpled
and unshaven.

Maybe someday I will forgive
negligence,
a careless inattention
to the upkeep of an earthen dam,
but I will never understand
the soul
of a man who could turn his back
on his own child.

I will never forgive Celestia's father.

Last time I saw him
I stood helpless in the shadows
as he wedged an ocean between
his daughter and me.

I can't imagine how he'll try to separate us this time.
I stand my ground.

He barely looks at me.
"Where is she?" He sizes up each huddled form.
Celestia's not one of them.
Finally I see his eyes,
red,
wet.

They bore right into me.
"Is she . . . ?"
His throat quivers.

I don't know how I have any pity left in me—
he just looks so broken—
and I know how much I wish my papa was looking for me.

I nod toward the tent.
He rushes past me.

Kate

The girl's daddy
carries on awhile,
like you don't expect from a grown man.
I just give them some privacy.
Then he comes out of the tent.
I tell him we'll know in a few days
and he says to me, "How can I ever thank you enough
for tending my daughter?"
He takes out his wallet.

If I live to be a hundred,
I will never understand rich folks.

Still, what's left of my pride
would like to chew on his gratitude for a bit,

but I hear myself saying, "The boy here's the one."
The daddy just stands there,
mouth open,
wallet open. . . .
What now?

Peter

I'm not sure I hear right—
I saw Kate take care of Celestia with my own eyes.
Kate stares me down and nods.
"He didn't leave her side.
Set up with her all night."

Well, *that* I did.
Told stories
and what I could remember of the old songs
Mama used to sing
when I was small
and had a fever.
I just did what I thought Mama would do.

"He watched over her every breath.
You couldn't have done better yourself."
Kate has a way,
so matter-of-fact—
you can't disagree with her.

"I've ordered a train car"—
Mr. Whitcomb checks his pocket watch—
"to take her home.
I'll get her the best doctors in Pittsburgh."
He's going to take her away!
I can't lose her again.
I start to say that she belongs here,
that she chose to come here,
but *here* is such a bad bet.
Better that she lives.
I nod. "Just let me say goodbye."

"I need your help getting her to the train"—
Mr. Whitcomb scratches the new whiskers on his chin—
"and later."
I half wonder if my hearing's been affected.
Kate nudges my shoulder.
"Okay."

Kate hands me the stretcher.
"There'll still be plenty of work to do
when you get back."
What's that flicker—
is Kate about to smile?
But I see
it is the fighting-back-tears kind of smile.

Celestia is safe.

Clean dry blankets,
velvet-cushioned seats,
a private train car.
The fever breaks.
She sleeps.
Her father and I stare at each other.
He motions to sit.
Does he really mean for me to stay?
It'll be a long ride to Pittsburgh.

Porters hurry in with silver trays:
hot tea,
hot biscuits,
cream,
meat.
"Eat." He jabs a fork in the direction of my plate.
I don't want to accept his food.
I don't want to be beholden,
but my stomach has other ideas.
I had forgotten my hunger
until I smelled food.
My knees buckle
and I sit without meaning to.

He reacts the same way.
Dives into the food
and signals the porter for more.
I must look shocked

because he stops and wipes his chin.
"I haven't eaten for days either.
As soon as the dam went out,
I knew that I wouldn't stop until I found her."

The words fly out
before I can stop myself: "She thought she was disowned."

Mr. Whitcomb swallows and nods,
pushing his plate away. "On the way to Johnstown,
not knowing if she was even alive . . ."—
he inhales deeply—
"whole towns were . . . demolished,
families separated.
I helped them look
for the . . . bodies,
their children."
Mr. Whitcomb covers his face,
rubs his eyes,
and goes on.
"What would any of those parents give
to have their child back?
Would they trade obedience?
Money?
Power?
The good opinion of their friends?"
He looks directly at me now.
"Absurd to even ask, right?
They're just words."

He looks like he's waiting
for me to agree,
or maybe to forgive.
I look away,
but with a nod.

We look down over Johnstown
from the train
as it crosses the stone bridge.
He shrugs in the direction
of the destruction below.
"So much senseless loss . . .
how could anyone
choose
to lose someone he loves?"

Kate

An older woman marches
into my camp.
She is neat,
compact,
all business.
She sizes up my work.

Strangers trail behind her.
From the horrified looks on their faces,

I gather they have just arrived in Johnstown.
The woman waves her hand
and the strangers begin passing boxes
and stacking them.

I step into her path,
but she already has me in her sights.
"I assumed you were a folktale," she says. "I'm pleased
to see you with my own eyes."
"I beg your pardon?"
"Miss Barton, Red Cross." She nods
and clasps my hand briefly. "Stories of your courage
and hard work have reached every city in the United States."
"People shouldn't be wasting their energy
talking about me
when there's so much work to be done."
"That's what I said.
But I can see"—
she folds her hands over her skirts—
"you have done quite a bit already.
We brought you some supplies."
I return her stare. "I have my own way of doing things."
"No strings attached, of course.
I'll let you get back to work."
She turns and waves her group onward.

At the edge of my camp,
she calls over her shoulder, "My office is a railcar.
Come by when you're ready to talk about combining our efforts."

I wait until she is out of sight
before I rip into the boxes.

❧

Hadn't given it much thought:
just figured the job out east wouldn't wait forever,
that this detour meant I was needed here
indefinitely.

But what about after that?
Help rebuild Johnstown, yes,
but stay on and call it home?
Nurse for a local doctor?
Dresser in a hospital?
Can I ever go back
to that life?

No.
The right thing to do
is to go where I am needed most,
wherever in the world that may be.

When our work in Johnstown is done,
I will kick out the coals of my fire,
grab the little ax
and the chipped pot—
these are truly useful objects—
and go to the railcar with the red-and-white sign.

"Good," she will say,
plain, not smug,
and she will direct me to the work that requires my hand.
Miss Barton is a woman who knows the natural order of things—
same as me—
and the natural thing
is for me to team up with the Red Cross.

East Conemaugh

Maura

I'm making a new patchwork now,
pieces of the lives of strangers uphill:
part of a roof,
half of a barn door,
other planks,
all washed down from Mineral Point,
or South Fork, maybe.
They look like treasures compared to nothing.
I drag them over to where I think our house used to be
and assemble
a makeshift shelter
for the children to toddle in and out of,
to keep the rain off when we sleep.

My knuckles are split,
my palms full of splinters.

I picture a family in Johnstown below
using pieces of our house for the same purpose—
or maybe even
airing out a shred of my quilt?
But I'm not mourning it.
I don't even want it back.
The story has changed.
I see us for what we are:
a child bride
with babies one after the other after the other,
too close together,
and a husband more than twice her age,
who loves his family
and loves his work,
but
who might not have a choice
about entering this new life,
this
consuming
public
life.
Alone.

I had decided to share Joseph
if I must,
but,

truth is,
he belongs to them now.
They are the ones to decide
how much to share him
with me.

Not a story I should like to tell,
nor a quilt I should like to make.

Pittsburgh

Celestia

Peter reads aloud to me,
same as every evening
since we arrived in Pittsburgh.
He lingers over the last line,
closes the book,
and stirs the fire.
I raise the fur-trimmed blanket to my chin
as he sits at the foot of the chaise longue.

"What should we read next?"
Peter scans the wall of books behind me.
"You choose," I say.

I care only for the sound of his voice,
reassuring me that he is really here,
a guest in my parents' home—
parents who claim and defend me.

We are warm and dry.
We have plenty to eat
and my health will be completely restored
after a few weeks' rest.
We are together.
Mother,
Father,
Peter,
and me.
If only it were not too late for Estrella—
I will never forget my vow to find her.
If only I knew where to begin,
or if only Mimsy would return and offer a clue.
But we have not heard a word
in all this time.
Estrella may be beyond our reach,
never hearing of Father's change of heart.
Will he try to locate her?
To tell her?
Even so, could she ever forgive him?
Is she lost to us forever?

The volunteer ladies have taken over the ballroom,
and so the house is filled with commotion,
chatter,
comings and goings,
gloves mislaid,
and enormous pots of tea.

When I arrived home,
I expected to find Mother
wracked with worry,
reclining on her fainting couch,
alternately waving smelling salts
and a silk fan,
complaining of vapors
or some such.
Instead I found a new version of Mother,
back straight,
jaw set,
quietly orchestrating a monumental relief effort
with a zeal in her eyes
that says
she was *saving me*
by bundling blankets,
coats,
foodstuffs,
by prying into the wallets and string purses
of our wealthy friends and neighbors,
and she would not stop or sleep or eat until

word came
of my safety.
Or demise.

⁂

Mother fusses
when I insist on helping the volunteers,
but I tire quickly anyway.
She helps me to a stuffed chair
where I cut lengths of string
for tying up bundles of blankets or clothing.
Peter is off exploring the library,
where we will meet later.

All the biddy hens are here:
Louise Godwin
and Lucille Marshall,
acting like the dam broke just to inconvenience them,
their whole crowd
kissing the ground they walk on.
They clear throats,
try not to look at me,
and busy themselves at the other end of the ballroom.
I can hear them just the same:
"What her parents must have suffered!"
"She could have been killed!"
"If she were mine, I wouldn't allow her back in the house!"
"Imagine, throwing her life away on that . . . urchin!"

My voice surprises us all: "His name is Peter."
All whispering stops and I sit upright.
"He watched over me when I was ill"—
I move toward them—
"and he is here
in this house
at my parents' invitation.
You are not welcome to speak of him this way."

Mother looks at me with alarm,
but then her new quiet strength takes over
and she comes to stand beside me,
leveling her stare at those gossips.
Mrs. Godwin smirks and exchanges glances with her friends.
"Think about what you're saying, my dear.
One word from me can bar the door
of every quality family on the Eastern seaboard."
"Speak it, then, if you must, Louise."
Mother hands me a blanket.
"We have more important work
to get on with."
We resume folding and stacking blankets.

Mrs. Godwin's mouth works with sounds she cannot utter—
Mother has rendered her speechless!

Mrs. Marshall glares down her bony nose
and steers Mrs. Godwin toward the door.
They stop after a few paces. "Ladies . . ."
A few women follow them,

a few look torn,
but a good number crowd around Mother,
nodding and reaching for bundling string.

I fold a blanket up high
to hide my smile.

Peter

My thoughts return to Johnstown,
to rebuilding,
to a home I could bring Celestia back to
once she's well.

"Stay for dinner tonight at least," the old man says.
"I have a special surprise planned for Celestia and her mother."

Celestia

Dinner is beautiful.
The candles glow gold,
the linens are starched crisp,
the silver shimmers,
the beef is tender,
the sauce savory.

My velvet gown,
wine, and good company
warm me.

"Your cheeks are pink." Peter smiles.
It brings me back
to our first days together
on the banks of Lake Conemaugh,
a lake that no longer exists.

Safe,
comfortable,
surrounded by people I love,
how I wish the same could be said
for the citizens of Johnstown,
who live with the scars
and high-water marks
of those three rivers,
whose search for lost loved ones
will never end.
I know what they feel.

I return Peter's smile,
but he must see the sadness in my eyes.
"Thinking of your sister?" he whispers.
I close my eyes,
nodding.

A clatter in the drive
threatens to disrupt

our peace—
not the first time word from the office
called Father away—
but Father is not grumbling
and checking his pocket watch.
He is grinning at Mother expectantly.

Realization sweeps over me
and I rise to my feet.
"Oh!" is all I manage to say.

Mother looks concerned. "Celestia, dear, what is it?"
Father chuckles.
Peter looks confused.

Laughing,
running,
throwing open the front door,
jumping the stairs,
I am upon the carriage even before it stops.

Estrella has come home.

She is laughing and crying.
We are hugging,
she holds my face in her hands.
"Thank heaven you were spared!"

I kiss her hands. "Thank heaven you are home."

At last,
everyone I love
under one roof.

And new people to love:
Estrella's new husband, Lord Edgar,
who introduces himself,
"I had been waiting
my whole dull life
to be struck
by love at first sight
the instant Estrella set foot
on British soil."
And darling Baby Henry,
a stout curly-headed fellow,
and Mimsy accompanying them all.

Mimsy pulls me aside
as she removes her gloves. "Edgar has a title and a castle
but he's poor as a churchmouse,
like so many of them are.
We worked out a little arrangement
with your father's banker." Mimsy winks.
"Father *knew*
where she was?"
"Oh, he always *knew* . . .
he could just never make contact,

left it to old Aunt Mimsy
to find a loophole."
"A loophole?"
"A flat-broke English country gentleman
willing to be swept away
by your sister's beauty and charm
before she even had need to let out her corset."
"And she loves him?"
"They're mad for each other.
See for yourself." Mimsy nods toward
the little group.

Estrella straightens Edgar's collar
and looks into his eyes.
He gently replaces a stray curl for her
and smiles.
Mother nuzzles the baby.
I am satisfied.

We are together at last,
snug under one roof.
This is the source of my strength,
the strength that will carry me
back to Johnstown
to face whatever challenges wait for me there
when I return with Peter.

Author's Note

When I was a kid, a bunch of friends and I were talking about how cool it would be if our houses were underwater. We could swim through the rooms like deep-sea explorers, swim or boat to each other's houses, and dive off the roofs. My dad happened to over-hear and he explained that it would be the opposite of cool. We asked, "Has this ever happened anywhere, a town underwater?" A history buff, my dad must have told me about the Johnstown flood, but I was too young to sense the gravity of it.

In high school, I saw a movie about the flood in history class. I couldn't get the story of class strata, power, and accountability out of my head for years. By the time I stumbled across the movie again on TV in the 1990s, I was thinking like a writer. I could picture so clearly the ladies in white reclining on the porch of the clubhouse, or strolling the boardwalk. *This would make a great novel!*

Early on, I intended that my completely fictitious characters would be mixed in with real people—for example, John Hess, the railroad engineer who warned East Conemaugh with his train whistle. When I chose to tell his story as seen through the eyes of his wife, the characters took on lives of their own, deviat-ing from the actual history. Following a thread like that, letting the story unfold in ways that surprise you, is the most enjoyable part of writing. Thus we have Maura, and Joseph, instead of John Hess.

Another case is Grayson. Although the wealthy industrialists Andrew Carnegie, Henry Clay Frick, and Andrew Mellon were club members, none of them fit the profile of the philandering tycoon too powerful to coerce into marriage. Grayson, young and more of a man-about-town, is a stand-in.

Then there's the real-life story of six-year-old Gertrude Quinn, who rode out the flood on a mattress. A man jumped in to help and literally threw her to rescuers in a saloon at the water's edge. This event inspired Celestia's ride and rescue.

So, as it turned out, I didn't place many real people in this novel, only events and situations inspired by them.

Amazing rescues, unlikely deaths, fascinating survival stories, and tales of the fickle nature of the wave—I wanted to squeeze every one into my story. But you can find them all in David McCullough's book *The Johnstown Flood.* I have read it many times by now and my respect for it increases with each pass. McCullough makes an enormous amount of information accessible and enjoyable to read. If you want to sit down with a book to learn more about the flood, this is the one. If you want to travel to Pennsylvania and get a firsthand look at the site, visit

- the Johnstown Flood Museum
  (www.jaha.org/FloodMuseum/history.html)
  and
- the Johnstown Flood National Memorial
  (www.nps.gov/jofl).

The remaining buildings of the South Fork Fishing and Hunting Club are in the village of St. Michael.

This is not a book *about* the flood. My intention was to tell a fictional story set against the backdrop of the flood. Time and geography are sometimes condensed to facilitate storytelling.

—J.R.

South Fork Dam Chronology

1830s: A reservoir of water is needed for the Johnstown-to-Pittsburgh section of Pennsylvania's river-fed canal system so that it does not run dry in the summer. A dam will hold back South Fork Creek, and its pipe valves will be controlled to allow a steady flow into the Johnstown basin by way of the Little Conemaugh River.

In preparation for the reservoir, 400 acres are cleared.

1838: Work begins on an earthen dam.
An earthen dam has three requirements:
1. A spillway must be cut through rock.
2. Discharge pipes must be provided.
3. Water must never be allowed to flow over the top.

A spillway is an outlet for excess water; this one is cut 72 feet wide through solid rock. Its purpose is to prevent overflow, but its appearance is that of a picturesque waterfall.

1852: Work is complete. The dam is over 900 feet across, 72 feet high, and 270 feet thick at its base. **South Fork Reservoir** begins to fill.

Progress by the Pennsylvania Railroad quickly puts the canals out of business.

1857: The Pennsylvania Railroad buys the canal system, including the dam, for rights-of-way.

The reservoir is unused, largely forgotten.

1862: The dam breaks due to a defect in the foundation.

Little damage is caused because the lake is at less than half capacity and a watchman in the tower opens the valves immediately, reducing pressure on the dam and releasing the water in a controlled fashion.

The watchtower burns down soon after.

The reservoir is barely a pond, again forgotten.

1875: Congressman John Reilly purchases the property, removes the discharge pipes, and sells them for scrap.

1879: The dam changes hands again, this time purchased by Benjamin Ruff on behalf of a private sportsmen's club. Membership list (revealed years later) includes:

Andrew Carnegie, iron and steel magnate, Carnegie, Phipps & Company;

Henry Clay Frick, the "Coke King," H. C. Frick Coke Company and chairman of Carnegie, Phipps & Company;

Philander C. Knox, lawyer for all Carnegie business;

Andrew Mellon, banker, T. Mellon & Sons;

Henry Phipps Jr., partner in Carnegie, Phipps & Company; and

Robert Pitcairn, head of the Pittsburgh Division of the Pennsylvania Railroad.

Ruff repairs the dam with rocks, brush, and even horse manure. The discharge pipes are not replaced. No one on-site has engineering credentials.

One month later, rain washes away most of the repairs.

1880: Engineer John Fulton is sent by Daniel J. Morrell, head of the Cambria Iron Works in Johnstown, to examine the dam. Fulton reports a leak at the location of the repairs. He recommends "a thorough overhauling" and "the construction of an ample discharge pipe."

Club president Ruff responds: ". . . you and your people are in no danger from our enterprise."

Cambria Iron offers to help *pay* for an overhaul. The club declines.

1881: More damage by rain.

Lake Conemaugh, estimated at 200 million tons, is stocked with one thousand black bass. Screens are installed over the spillway to prevent fish from escaping.

At some point, the height of the dam is lowered to widen the road for carriage traffic. Besides bringing the top of the dam that much closer to the water level, this reduces the capacity of the spillway.

Water is 2 feet from the breast of the dam.

   June 10: First rumor of the dam breaking.

Rumor repeats every year with heavy rains. It quickly becomes a running joke.

1885: Morrell dies.

1887: Ruff dies.

1889:
  May 30:
    11:00 p.m.: Heavy rain begins.
  May 31:
    6:00 a.m.: Rivers are rising 1 foot per hour.

    10:00 a.m.: Workers find they cannot remove the debris-clogged screens from the main spillway. They try cutting an emergency spillway through the opposite hill, but with little success.

    11:00 a.m.: Lake water is level with the top of the dam.

    The club sends a warning to the valley by telegraph. Lines are down and messages are delayed.

    12:00 noon: Rising river water in Johnstown is 2–10 feet deep.

    Decision is made *not* to cut another spillway through the dam itself.

    Telegraph operators in East Conemaugh and Johnstown receive messages from up the line warning that the dam might be breaking, like other messages in other years. They ignore them.

    12:30 p.m.: Water, 50–60 feet wide, starts over the center of the dam. Workers tear up the bridge over the spillway.

2:45 p.m.: Another telegraph warning is received by East Conemaugh and Johnstown.

A 10-by-4-foot hole appears in the top of the dam.

3:00 p.m.: First break.

3:10 p.m.: Dam is gone.

> **South Fork:** population 1,500 approximately.
>
> Town is built mostly on the hillside.
>
> Total deaths: 4.
>
> **Mineral Point:** population 200 approximately.
>
> Due to rising water, many residents had already moved to higher ground.
>
> Total deaths: 16.

3:46 p.m.: Reservoir is empty.

Later studies suggest it would have been like turning on Niagara Falls for 36 minutes.

> **East Conemaugh** and the train yards.
>
> Warning came from John Hess's train whistle.
>
> Total deaths of residents, including those of Franklin across the tracks: 28.
>
> Total deaths of train passengers: 22.
>
> **Woodvale:** population 1,000.
>
> No warning. Because the valley straightens out, the flood picked up speed.
>
> Total deaths: 314 (close to one in three people).

4:07 p.m.: Flood hits Johnstown.

> **Johnstown** and boroughs: population 30,000.
>
> Most damage is done in ten minutes.

Debris collects at the stone bridge; by nightfall it catches fire.

Many bodies were never found, but the generally accepted total of deaths is 2,209. Many of those found were unidentifiable.

June: Survivors organize quickly. Rescue efforts. Morgues.

Neighbors in the hills and surrounding towns are generous, opening their homes, sharing food.

Sightseers arrive with picnic baskets. Others arrive to help, but with no food or water or housing, they only increase the burden.

The American Red Cross with Miss Clara Barton arrives from Washington.

The Army arrives to help keep the peace.

June 10: First case of typhoid fever. Total deaths: 40.

Relief efforts all over the world bring in money, food, blankets, and clothes, anything people can spare.

July: First lawsuit filed against South Fork Fishing and Hunting Club. Individual negligence could not be proved.

September: Andrew Carnegie visits the flood site and offers to build a new library.

Source: *The Johnstown Flood* by David McCullough

Further Reading

Want to read more about the flood? Here are just some of the books you might enjoy. The Johnstown Area Heritage Association (www.jaha.org) online bookstore has additional titles. Except for the 1889 book from my family's personal collection, all the titles listed below should be available through local libraries.

Young Readers
Fiction:

Dahlstedt, Marden. *The Terrible Wave*. New York: Coward, McCann & Geoghegan, 1972.

Gross, Virginia T. *The Day It Rained Forever: A Story of the Johnstown Flood*. Once upon America series. New York: Viking, 1991.

Nonfiction:

Nobleman, Marc Tyler. *The Johnstown Flood*. We the People series. Minneapolis: Compass Point Books, 2006.

Stein, R. Conrad. *The Story of the Johnstown Flood*. Cornerstones of Freedom series. Chicago: Children's Press, 1984.

Adult Readers
Fiction:

Cambor, Kathleen. *In Sunlight, in a Beautiful Garden: A Novel*. New York: Farrar, Straus & Giroux, 2001; Harper Perennial, 2002.

Nonfiction:

Johnson, Willis Fletcher. *History of the Johnstown Flood*. Philadelphia: J. W. Keeler, 1889.

McCullough, David. *The Johnstown Flood*. New York: Simon & Schuster, 1968.

Acknowledgments

Enormous thanks to Patricia Reilly Giff, patient teacher, gentle critic, wise mentor, and gracious lady. Your beautiful Nory Ryan books gave me courage to start on my own journey to find a home with young readers. And your faith in my writing has been a miracle in my life. Thanks and love and blessings, Pat.

Thank you to my agent, George Nicholson, for sharing my vision of this book and for making a perfect match with the right editor, and to everyone involved at Sterling Lord Literistic. Many thanks go to Emily Hazel, formerly of SLL, for help in boiling down some early feedback on this book.

To my amazing editor, Joan Slattery: thank you, first of all, for taking on a big story crafted at the word level. Thank you for your guidance and support, and for your enthusiasm for my work. And thanks to everyone involved at Knopf.

Thanks go to the PEN New England Children's Book Caucus for choosing *Three Rivers Rising* as the Susan P. Bloom Discovery Award Winner for 2008: Susan P. Bloom, Pat Lowery Collins, Susan Goodman, Robie H. Harris, Lisa Jahn-Clough, Liza Ketchum, Lois Lowry, Leslie Sills, and Kim Ablon Whitney.

Readers of early versions of the manuscript: Dean Defino and Whitney Lok-Defino, Christine Peter, Penny Piva, Jennifer

Richards, Patricia Richards, Linda Richter, and Lisa Santiana. Thank you for the feedback and encouragement. And love. And snacks.

Thank you to my supportive group of fellow writers who watched this manuscript grow from its first baby steps to holding it in our hands right now: Pam Farley, Ann Haywood Leal, Gael Lynch, Christine Peter, Penny Piva, Patricia Richards, Bette Anne Rieth, MaryJo Scott, Laura Toffler-Corrie, and Margaret Welch; and to our Master of Ceremonies at The Dinosaur's Paw, Jimmy Giff.

Thank you to Sean Diamond for saving my life a little bit at a time.

Thank you to my parents for filling my head with history and books and ideas and dreams, the bricks and mortar of a book like this. Thanks for listening to my endless "what if" scenarios, then holding my feet to the fire when I just needed to "write it already." Your faith has never wavered.

Thank you to my daughters for never failing to repeat yourselves when I'm far away in the world of my story. Your love of books keeps me going, trusting that there *will* be a next generation of readers, and a next . . .

To my husband: only you truly know the extent of your sacrifices, to this book and to my dream of a writing life. Thank you for these gifts, as well as for your optimism and your love.

About the Author

Jame Richards's interest in history began with reluctance in childhood, when every school vacation involved a family trip in the paneled station wagon to museums, presidential tombs, and historical monuments. She bided her time until reaching the gift shop, wondering why she couldn't go to an amusement park or the beach like everyone else. During those long car trips, she learned to write and revise stories in her head. Twenty years of creative writing (sometimes even on paper) and her knowledge of history come together in *Three Rivers Rising*, her first novel. Prior to publication, *Three Rivers Rising* won the PEN New England Children's Book Caucus Susan P. Bloom Discovery Award, given to an unpublished work.

Jame Richards lives with her family in Connecticut.